THE
DARK
AND
LONELY
ROAD

A NOVEL

THE DARK AND LONELY ROAD

A NOVEL

SEAN GATES

"The Dark and Lonely Road" is a work of fiction. Any real persons are used fictitiously, and any words or actions attributed to them are not intended to represent their actual conduct. Wherever possible, real places, businesses, and historical events have been used to create the backdrop for the story. In some cases, real persons or businesses have been replaced with fictional ones in service of telling a crime story set in a real-life small town. On no account is any part of this work meant to implicate real persons, living or dead, in the commission of any criminal activities. Cogbill is the name of some of my relatives from Chesterfield, Virginia. Hieronymus is entirely fictitious.

First Printing: 2019

ISBN 978-0-359-44038-2

Used Books
PO Box 352 Dahlgren, VA, 22448
www.therationaldissident.com

ACKNOWLEDGEMENTS

THE LIST of people to whom I owe thanks for this novel is long, and should I omit anyone I apologize in advance:

Thanks to my readers, for the support and encouragement. Clayton Spinney, Grant Wilson, Kristy Mikos, and Christopher Stanton for the insight and advice, and especially the honesty. My friends and colleagues at Project94, Neil Richard, Sarah Snow, and Jeremy Bertz, for nudging me to write the article that ultimately inspired this novel, and for the feedback along the way. Erin Scroggs, for believing in me and reminding me to believe in myself.

Elizabeth Nuckols Lee, Peggy Mullen, Sandra Conner, and Gene Clift, for the history lessons -- any mistakes or inaccuracies are entirely my own. The good people at the Lewis Egerton Smoot Memorial Library, for fetching dusty tomes out of some unseen dungeon at my every request, and the Clerk of the Court's Office for pointing me in the right direction out of the gate.

As always, thanks to my brother Mahesh Raj Mohan, for setting me on this path a long time ago; my parents Rob and Beverly, my brother Darek McGee, and my sister Sinay Ou, for their love and support. Lina Zayas for giving me that last little push across the finish line.

Finally a special thanks to Mr. James, whoever you were, for walking here.

CHAPTER ONE

THE DAY I lost my job, the whistle blew for the first of two breaks and since the weather was good, most of the workers stepped outside to smoke cigarettes and make up stories about their personal lives. Even when the weather was poor I usually came outside for the fresh air and a glimpse of the sun, and to escape the endless clatter of the machines on the production floor. The less I had to talk to anyone the better I felt about them.

The blacks kept to themselves on one side of the lot, and the whites on the other. The whites were ignorant and spoke contemptuously of the blacks. The blacks feared the whites and knew better than to show it. I had nothing to say to the whites and I figured the blacks had nothing to say to me. One of the whites, a mechanic named Glenn, stalked over and asked me for a light.

"Sorry," I said. I have never cared to smoke.

He grinned and with his chin indicated the circle of black men laughing amongst themselves.

"What you suppose them boys're talking 'bout?"

"Probably the same as your buddies, bragging on their favorite baseball teams and lying about sex."

"Maybe."

He stood there a while watching them, until a couple of

the guys noticed him looking and took on a more serious posture. I looked at Glenn. He was thin as a scarecrow in baggy work pants and a short-sleeved shirt with buttons and a pocket on the left breast. His belt had a couple of extra notches that had been scraped out with an awl, his hair was lank and oily, and his skin looked sallow and dry, like if you braced him it would slide off in your hands.

"You should come sit with us, Cogbill. You never know what might happen."

"I'm fine right here, Glenn."

"Don't get me wrong, I ain't bias or nothing. You just never know what's on a nigra's mind."

I wasn't looking at him. Out near the edge of the forest, I thought I saw a man in army fatigues moving silently through the brush. I looked briefly to Glenn, and then back, and the man in the forest was gone.

"I like to be alone, Glenn. On my break. Do you mind?"

He regarded me with an expression close to pity, as though I were the ignorant one and not he. "You too good to hang around the rest of us, Cogbill?"

"No."

"You allergic to smoke?"

"Just bullshit."

"You ought to stick close to your own kind."

"I was trying to."

He looked puzzled for a moment, trying to decide if I'd just insulted him. Then he grinned and walked away.

Mount Rose, or the Pickle Factory as it was colloquially known, was a big white cinder block building, long and low, the interior a hot, high-ceilinged space full of clattering machinery that shat pickles into glass jars, pissed the jars full of brine, capped and sealed them, and glued a label around them. I wore a hairnet and a coverall and watched jars go sliding by me on conveyors.

The pneumatic hammering sound was like machinegun fire. It kept me bound up with the creaking sense of impending calamity associated with an old rope bed: I always seemed to be one good torque away from implosion. Usually I managed to spare people the worst, biting out words like a mountain lion biting the throat out of a fawn. Often they didn't deserve it. Sometimes they did.

It wasn't a surprise when I got called into the plant manager's office that afternoon, a sort of disembodied interior like a movie set built in a warehouse space, windows all around so The Man could survey his domain. He had a battered metal desk and a threadbare office chair, and waved me impatiently to a seat opposite him.

"All right, what did I do now?"

"Dial it down, Cogbill. It's your mouth gets you in trouble. I swear it's like you don't want to be here."

"We make pickles, Mike."

"And we take pride in it."

"Who takes pride in fucking pickles?"

"Don't walk in my office and start swearing at me."

"Does anyone even like pickles? For Christ's sake, it's a stunted cucumber in a jar of piss."

"I think you have a problem, Harold. I think you don't belong here, and I think you know it. Your attitude is just plain disrespectful."

"I wasn't swearing at you, Carl. We were talking about pickles."

"You damn well know when you were in the Army you wouldn't talk to your superiors like that."

"Of course I did, Carl, it was the goddamn Army. How do you think we talked?"

"Why do you keep calling me Carl?"

"Why do you keep calling me Harold?"

"Get your things out of your locker and get out. Did they seriously let you get away with this stuff in the Army?"

"No. They kicked me out."

Mike put his hands up in the air, popped his eyes and shook his head. The conversation was over. I dropped my hairnet in a jar of pickles on my way off the production floor.

It was late summer 1959, and I was living in King George County: a dusty, mainly forgotten saddle-shaped piece of Virginia in the bend of the Potomac river an hour south of Washington, DC. I did not yet understand the condition that kept me awake at nights, often until dawn, in my creaky little farmhouse at the end of a mile-long dirt drive. I do believe that certain events in our lives are ordained by a higher power and are as unavoidable as the sunrise, but I had no idea that such an event was about to occur. Should I claim otherwise it would be an untruth, no matter how romantic.

It was late August and Wednesday night gave slow, painful birth to an unwelcome Thursday morning. I was sitting at my kitchen table, staring at the wall clock, listening to a beetle slam itself into my window-screen. The bare fixture in my ceiling was like a neon nautilus, its pale, sterile light an island in the darkness that seemed to have engulfed my life. I debated going to bed, but it was already pushing five-thirty and there seemed little point. The coffee in my cup had grown cold, and the percolator had long-since ceased its flatulence. I disassembled it, rinsed it out, and started a fresh pot.

I started a pot for grits, and opened a can of corned-beef hash, neither of which I'd had the distinct pleasure of doing in the Pennsylvania diner where I had been employed some years before. I used milk in my grits, rather than water. Heresy I know, but I preferred the creamier flavor.

I beat milk and eggs in a cereal bowl using a stainless-steel salad fork, and added a little crushed red pepper from a yellow and red container marked SAUER'S in block text. I poured my eggs in the skillet beside the hash. By the time the grits set I could stand my spoon upright in the bowl as the butter melted around it.

I stuffed all the pots and pans in the sink – a problem for another time – and after breakfast took the rest of my coffee on my sagging gallery porch, watching as the broken egg-yolk sun oozed all over the treetops and burned off the lingering fog across the field.

The bark of a fox kit stuttered somewhere in the brush. What I called a yard had been a small farm just a few years before, and a few old fences cut it into pens. The fences were covered in Virginia creeper and wild grape, and the fields, gone to seed, were choked with weeds and wildflowers. I wondered if the fox's mother was out there somewhere, but I didn't hear any reply. The foxes would all be going to bed for the day, but the kit in my yard croaked out another series of wow-wow-wow's. Maybe a runt. Abandoned, or injured in training for the hunt. Natural selection.

I heard the truck before I saw it. A rolling cloud of dust tumbled up the dirt road and parted the fields like Moses parting the sea. It was a dusty, battered, decade-old Ford, pontoon fenders and running boards, the morning sun like the glory of God streaming off the chrome. The woman who got out was wearing denim bib overalls and a flannel shirt with the sleeves rolled to her elbows. She was round-shouldered and her hair was short, curled inward around her ears and neck. She was not pretty, but she went well with the truck.

"You Harold Cogbill?"

"No, but then who is."

"I heard you were a smart-aleck."

"The name's Hieronymus," I said. "But you can call me Harry, it's easier on both of us."

"Look, cut it with the funny business, I need your help."

I needed more coffee. Or possibly less coffee and more sleep.

I said, "help? With what?"

"Something damn peculiar is going on at my uncle's place and I need someone to look into it."

I tried to do the math and came up empty.

"Begging your pardon, ma'am, but it's early yet and I'm only on my sixth cup of coffee, so it's possible I'm missing something. What is it you think I do for a living?"

"Currently unemployed, is what I heard."

"I'll grant that's true."

"So you'll do it?"

"What? No--? Let's start this over." I set my tin cup on the railing, stepped down and stuck my hand out. "Morning, miss. My name's Harry. And you would be...?"

"Ethel Burkitt. You used to be a cop, ain't that right?"

"What lying son of a bitch told you that?"

"Well, John over at the post office on account of he seen a envelope addressed to Mister Harry Cogbill from the Massachusetts Department of Corrections, and he remembered you said you used to deal with prisoners and all."

"John's got it turned around. I was a guard, that's all. I'm sorry."

The fox kit was crying now.

Miss Ethel Burkitt got back in her truck, turned it around in the dirt loop in front of my house, and took her cloud of dust back out to Gera Road. I stepped back up on my drooping porch, the old planks creaking beneath my feet, and resumed my cup. The coffee had gone cold, and the fox kit's crying had grown more pitiful. I stood there, watching the birds pecking at the ground and the butterflies bobbing drunkenly among the blooms in the yard. A single turkey buzzard had taken up his circling watch above the field. I tossed the cold coffee into the grass, put the cup back on the railing, and walked out across the field toward the sound of the crying fox.

He was a little thing, not even cat-sized, blue eyes, white-and-black on his stubby little muzzle, his back all grey, a black stripe down the top of his tail. The fur on his cheeks and around his ears had the faintest hint of red. He didn't fight me when I picked him up and carried him into the house. I opened a can of potted meat, put it in a cereal bowl and set it on the floor near the fox. Then I went and took a shower, brushed my teeth and put on fresh clothes.

I asked the fox if he wanted to go for a ride, and since he didn't say no, we got in my rust-streaked Hudson and headed for the store in Gera. I parked in the gravel, picked up my new friend, and stepped up onto the porch under the Coca-

Cola button signs and through the screen door into the musty little shop. The unpolished hardwood had absorbed a lifetime of dirt and seemed determined to do the same to the cold light of the fluorescents hanging from the rafters. The store, like most of the ones around the county in those days, was a holdover from an earlier era. He sold Cokes and Moon Pies and bags of sugar, flour, and dry dog food. I wasn't sure what to feed a fox. We selected a bag of Purina and took it to the counter.

John said hi to me and regarded my companion with some disdain.

"Better to let nature take its course," he said.

"Depends whose nature," I said.

"God's, usually." He wrote out prices on a ledger and punched in the numbers on a big bronze National register, then pulled my mail out of a cubby.

"Say, John, you didn't happen to suggest to a lady recently that I might be able to help her with some family trouble?"

"No sir, I don't reckon I'd frame it quite that way."

"Ethel Burkitt seems to recall a different series of events."

"When she was in here yesterday, she did say she thought her uncle might be in some trouble and I did mention how you used to be a policeman up in Boston, but that's all there was to it."

"I was never a policeman, John. I was a prison guard. There's a whole universe of difference. Why can't she just call the Sheriff?"

"Sheriff cain't help her if there ain't been no crime."

"I'll grant that's true."

The little fox in my arms listened to the whole conversation and didn't make a peep. But he looked as bored with it as I was.

"You ain't really gonna keep a gray fox for a pet, is you?"

"I guess I'm just a sucker," I said. "Miss Burkitt hasn't got a telephone, has she?"

CHAPTER TWO

MY CAR was only six years old, but I'd gotten it secondhand and the previous owner had not been kind to it. I always suspected he'd used it as a target for batting practice. Or opening coconuts, it could go either way. In any case it was full of dings, the paint had gone chalky with a lack of wax, and the rust from the chrome had streaked and spread to the sheet metal, blistering the robin's egg enamel like celluloid that lingered too long in front of the lamp. The roof was supposed to be white, and some of it still was.

I rattled down the long orange wheel-ruts and over a cattle guard as I entered the Burkitt property. I could see a whitewashed frame house up ahead of me, the sun blasting off the tin roof, an Aermotor windmill ginning in the field, and a little way behind it a big grey barn, the roof purple with rust. I wasn't really sure why I was there, but since I'd been fired from the cannery, I guess I needed something to do.

The little Hornet coupe creaked and banged up the Burkitt's driveway. A man I assumed was Ethel's father was driving a tractor in the field. He was wearing brown work pants and suspenders, a blue shirt open halfway down his chest, his sleeves rolled up off his wrists. Whatever was on his head probably used to be a panama hat. He stared balefully at me as I bumped along, then swerved and pulled his tractor up opposite me on the other side of the fence. I stopped, and he motioned for me to roll my window down.

"Can I help you, son?"

"Name's Harry, I'm here to see Miss Ethel."

"She know you're coming?"

"No sir, I'd have called ahead but was somewhat daunted by the fact that your telephone doesn't exist."

"A comedian," he said, and spit tobacco into the grass. "Alright, son, pull on up and I'll meet you in front of the house. Just so we're clear, Ethel doesn't want to see you, you get right back in that car and go. You got any trouble following directions and the doctors in town'll be digging buckshot out of your backside."

"Understood."

"The hell kind of dog is that?"

"Fox."

"Christ, Ethel."

I did as her old man said. I didn't really begrudge him his attitude. He was protecting his daughter, and I didn't figure she got a lot of gentlemen callers. Or whatever the hell I was, for that matter. I don't know how many years I had on her, but I was forty and she was not. I made her about mid-twenties. I left the fox in the car, with the windows open a little, and followed Mr. Burkitt around the back of the house to a chicken coop. Ethel was there with a bucket, spreading feed, in her overalls and flannel, neoprene boots, sort of a weird sack of girl, and when he called her name she turned, squinting in the sun, and threw a hand up to shade her eyes. She wore no hat, and the sun had turned her light brown hair to gold. When she saw me, she put the bucket down and her hand on her hip. Her whole posture changed.

"Why Harry Cogbill," she said.

"You know this man?"

"We met briefly," she said.

"He said he wanted to see you."

"He thinks he's funny."

"I've noticed. Does he stay or go?"

"Oh it's all right, daddy. We're going to take a walk, if you don't mind. We won't be a few minutes."

"You sure?"

"He ain't hurting nobody, and you know I can holler loud as anyone."

Ethel Burkitt wasn't exactly pretty, but I found myself looking at her. She had kind of a round face, big blue eyes and a spray of freckles across her nose. Her mouth pouted. She wiped her arm across her forehead and it left a smear of dirt.

Her father went out front to his tractor as Ethel and I strolled around the grounds. It was a pretty nice place, and I said so.

"Cut the crap, Harry Cogbill. What in the hell are you doing here?"

"As I recall, you wanted my help."

"As I recall, you made it pretty clear where I could go."

"I had...last night was...it's been a rough twenty years or so."

"Welcome to planet earth, Mr. Cogbill. You know what I think? I think you was setting up all night feeling sorry for yourself on account of you lost your job, and a little ol' farm girl in an overall and pickup truck come asking for help, and you figure your calendar's pretty full up what with all the mop-ing and the drinking and such."

"I hadn't been drinking," I said.

THE DARK AND LONELY ROAD | 15

She folded her arms across her chest, and squinted up at me as the wind blew her hair around. She dropped her voice as low as it would go and said, "look at me, I'm Harry Cogbill, you know what I do for a living? Not a damn thing, huh-huh-huh."

"I had that coming," I said.

"What, you're just gonna roll over? What happened to that smart mouth of yours?"

I thought it may have recognized its better, but I didn't say so. "I didn't come here to fight."

"Sure you did, just not with me."

"What the hell's that supposed to mean?"

"Well if you don't know, I'm sure not gonna tell you."

Christ, what had I gotten into? She brought the hand back up to her brow and her piercing blue eyes regarded me from the band of shade it created there.

"So now what," she said. "You just changed your mind?"

"Something like that, yeah."

"It ever occur to you that maybe I changed mine?"

"That's what I'm here to find out, isn't it?"

She shook her head. "I think you're here to find out what kind of man you are, cos you don't know, and that scares you."

"Will you stop trying to scramble my wires?"

"Probably not," she said, and grinned.

She had an uncanny ability to jab me right in the tender spots with an accuracy that would have shamed a championship fencer. It was as if she could read my heart, and I found it oddly comforting, if infuriating.

"So, what's your daily rate?"

I said, "My what?"

"You didn't think I expected you to work for free, did you?"

"I...well, I'm not sure."

"All you private investigators got a daily rate."

The grasshoppers were flying in from the field, gold shapes in the sunlight riding the smell of the mown grass like a thousand tiny kites on the wind.

"Miss Ethel, maybe you hadn't been listening, I'm not a private investigator."

"Well I'm hiring you to investigate, and I reckon that makes you a private investigator."

"Investigators got a license, you know, a Photostat in their wallet, says they're allowed to investigate."

"Mr. Cogbill, you know what a license is?"

"Didn't I just tell you?"

"It's when the government takes away your freedom to do something and then sells it back to you." Then she said, "If it's all the same to you, I'd rather not discuss the particulars here. Can I meet you this evening?"

"Miss Ethel, I believe I'd like to take you to dinner."

She shook her head and looked away from me, then stopped walking and turned her body to face me full-on.

"What did it for you, Mr. Cogbill? Was it the overalls, the chicken droppings on my boots or the sweat in my hair?"

I've always been hard-headed. I wasn't sure of a safe way to respond to that, so I grabbed her waist and kissed her. At first I thought she was going along with it, but then she started struggling and I let her go, and she slapped me. Just slapped the hell right out of me.

I stood there looking at the ground, my hand on my neck, my face burning.

She said, "all right."

"All right what?"

"All right, Mr. Harry Cogbill, you can take me to dinner."

"Well hot damn."

"You better believe it."

I drove home and put a bowl of water down for the fox, and opened a Coke for myself. My hands were shaking and my feet wouldn't stay still. I had a job and a date. Probably I'd get back there to pick her up and find out she'd changed her mind about all of it; no job, no date. Then her father would shoot me in the ass and the natural order of the universe would be restored. But the sudden burst of energy didn't go away. I did the dishes. I mopped the floors. I cleaned my toilet bowl and did the wash and hung it out to dry in the back yard. I thought I ought to take a nap. I laid down a while but I was wired. The fox, on the other hand, had been up well past his bedtime, and after a drink of water he slinked under my bed and went right to sleep.

I picked Miss Ethel up around seven o'clock. She was on the porch in a blue dress, sleeveless with a high, wide neckline and a tapered waist, and a crocheted shrug. She was in heels and stockings with a seam up the back of the leg, and she had a clutch and her hair was curled. Her face was made up, in a way that effectively highlighted her eyes, and she had a little bracelet and a locket. I had incorrectly estimated her it seemed in more ways than one. If she had, that morning, looked like a girl in a denim sack, I now somewhat envied the sack. I had put on a tie, and a vest, and my least-battered pair of oxfords, and I had the presence of mind to get out and open her car door.

"Hello, Miss Ethel."

"Hello yourself, Harold Cogbill."

"Hieronymus."

She laughed.

"Wait, that's really your name? Dear Lord, I thought you were putting me on."

"Does this mean it's over?"

"I'll let you know." She grinned.

I closed her door for her, then walked back around and got behind the wheel.

"Where did you get this car, Hieronymus Cogbill?"

"I bought it from King Kong, I guess he was tired of slamming it around."

"I don't think he was tired, I think he was finished."

"You may be on to something."

"I don't know where you were planning to take me, Cogbill, but I do have a suggestion."

"I thought Fredericksburg, there's nothing really out here."

"Oh don't let's drive into town, Harry Cogbill, let's go up to Dahlgren. There's a place up there we can eat and besides, I'd like to show you something near there."

"Not Wilkerson's."

"The Potomac Grill? What's wrong with that, Mr. Fussybritches?"

"Fussybritches?"

"That's a thing, go along with it."

"Sure. Well, I used to be a cook, and—"

"Now don't start with that, it's far too soon to get me into your house."

I felt my face burning again.

"That's not...Good Lord, Miss Ethel. I wasn't suggesting..."

"Careful you don't hurt my feelings. Maybe it really was the overalls."

"I like you very much, Miss Ethel."

"I like you too, Harry Cogbill."

I drove us to Route 3, and past the pickle factory out to 301. There was an old brick house with a tin roof on one corner, with an outbuilding and a low brick wall bordering the grounds by the road, the ruins of a colonial estate called Office Hall. An auto repair shop called Garrison's stood on another corner. I eased out onto 301 and turned left, toward Dahlgren.

A few miles on there was a traffic circle at Edgehill where Ridge Road crossed 301, a red-brick store with a metal awning called Circle Market on the left. A left on Ridge, or route 205, would head back to Gera at a place called Purkins' Corner, while a right led to Colonial Beach. Which would also have been a much better night out than going to the Potomac Grill up in Dahlgren. I didn't know what Ethel had in mind making me take her there, but every time I asked her she just told me wait and see.

We passed Ralph Bunche School where Eden Drive crossed 301 and became Hanover Church Road. The schools were still segregated, then, and this was the big new school they'd built for the black kids to prolong the inevitable integration. There was a fire tower behind the schoolyard, overlooking the scrubby forests and the orange dirt of the softball field, and its placement always struck me as unintentionally symbolic.

We rose and fell over the gently rolling hills, through woodland and fields, past places where the old road had been straightened and the former right-of-way given names like Ivy Hill and Will Loop. Near Owens we passed a red-brick motel with a matching diner in front, a plain black sign calling out the name, Hillcrest.

Then all at once the road dropped away and the view opened wide before us, a huge crater from some ancient meteor strike. We coasted down the long, steep hill toward the intersection with Dahlgren Road far below, the red-and-white checkered water towers of the Navy base visible beyond the trees, the shimmering ribbon of the Potomac just beyond the edges of our sight. The setting sun was to our left, and the sky was the color of the first peaches of spring behind periwinkle cumulus etched in flame.

At the bottom of the hill a white frame house and a barn sat away from the road behind a wedge-shaped field in the northern crotch of the intersection. Away above the trees on the ridge line to our left, Cloverdale House kept watch, its face split by a red brick chimney. Dahlgren Road came on at an acute angle from the left, back up the hill through Owens, from Arnold's Corner west of the courthouse.

To the right ahead of us it bridged over Upper Machodoc Creek and swept south to the main gate at the Naval Weapons Laboratory. We stayed on 301, the land low and boggy beyond the intersection, reedy creeks and marshes snaking off the Potomac into the countryside, the air faintly septic on a warm summer evening.

"Up here on the left," she said. "About a mile."

"The service station?"

"That's my uncle's place."

"So you want to hire me because something funny is going on at a gas station?"

"Not the gas station, the airfield."

"Okay, I'll bite."

There was an air field behind the filling station, sitting on a lot probably north of 150 acres.

"Just some strange characters. I commented as to how I don't like the people been around lately, and Uncle Jack said not to be so unwelcoming of outsiders."

"He's got a point. I'm an outsider."

"He hasn't got a point, Hieronymus Cogbill, I've been very damned nice to you."

"That's true, you did not have to come out with me tonight."

"I certainly did not."

We were coming up on it now, but the sun was about spent down in the hollow depression below Owens Drive, and there wasn't much to see in any case; the air field in question was all grass, and only the filling station had any lights. We crossed Williams Creek, the shadows deepening among the trees lining the two-lane highway, and then passed Gate B of the Dahlgren base where Owens Drive and 614 met at 301.

Wilkerson's Potomac Grill was a little further up, on the left, a little diner with two sets of paned windows and a kind of turret in the middle framing the door. The top of the building, just below the flat roof, had a sort of false crenellation that ran the length of the façade, and a tall neon sign by the entrance to the parking lot called out the establishment, "POTOMAC

GRILL – SEA FOOD – FINE FOOD" and in red, "OPEN." There was a clock on the turret, above the door.

We parked around the right corner, near three windows with awnings. When we opened the car doors, the sound of frogs in the marshland around us rippled through the night air, nearly coruscant. I didn't mind diner food or country nights, but I thought maybe we were a little overdressed, and for a first date I'd hoped to impress Ethel a little. This was not impressive, but as we walked around the gravel lot and I admired Ethel in the neon glow; she caught me looking and smiled. Well, all right.

Through the aluminum storm door was the basic tile floor, Formica tabletops with chrome trim and vinyl seats. The walls were wood-paneled and a counter ran across the far end of the room, with the kitchen behind it. I put my fedora on a coat tree by the door. There were one or two other couples, a small group of teenagers, and two or three old guys at the counter.

In the corner farthest from the door and away from all the windows, were three guys in ill-fitting grey sport coats and sloppy neckties, and one of them hadn't bothered to remove his hat. They looked a little rough; something about the set of their jaws and the hardness of their eyes. Having been a corrections officer, and a bond enforcer, I felt like I knew hoods when I saw them, and these guys were setting off all sorts of alarm bells. Highway 301 was a major traveler's route, though, and weekends this time of year it tended to jam up pretty bad. It was only Thursday, but maybe they were just passing through.

I didn't spend any undue amount of time looking at them, I just noticed, filed it away, and kept going. I tried to steer Ethel to a booth well away from those guys, but it turned out I didn't have to. We stayed near the front in the opposite corner of the room, and she purposely put me so I was facing them and she wasn't.

"See those guys in the corner, Mr. Cogbill? Look but don't look like you're looking."

"I already saw them."

"Those are the guys."

"I think I see the problem."

"I thought you might. Still think I'm just a crazy li'l farm girl?"

"I never thought that."

"Begging your pardon, Hieronymus, but who's the lyin' son of a bitch now?"

I grinned. She grinned back.

"Okay," I said. "What do we do now?"

"Now you buy me dinner, drive me home, give me a really dynamite kiss goodnight, and tomorrow, you get to work."

When I got home that night I didn't go right to sleep. I was exhausted after about thirty-six hours awake, but my mind was racing, thinking about all the things I might have done wrong and whether Miss Ethel would go out with me again, or more absurdly if she'd somehow maneuvered me into taking her out so that she could lead me past the airfield and show me the guys in the diner. Even the soothing sounds of the country night outside my open window didn't put me under. I tossed and turned until the sheet was tangled around my legs, then angrily kicked it off and gave up on sleep. I got dressed and made a pot of coffee, then dumped it out and went back to bed.

The trouble with being happy is I know it won't last, and I always manage to talk myself out onto a ledge. I kept wondering why Ethel hadn't hollered when I'd kissed her that first time. Her daddy would have laid me out, or run me off the property and out of the county and possibly the next one, and thus onward until he drove me into the sea. Maybe she really did like me. Or maybe it had been an act to get me to come work for her. Maybe I was the mark in some elaborate scam.

The fox kit jumped onto the bed, nipped playfully at my hand. I rubbed his belly and he rolled around with one eye closed, mouth open in a wide smile. Eventually he got his feet under him, stood up, squeaked out a rasping bark, and raced off into the darkened house. I waited for the inevitable sound of something breaking, knowing it would come; and when at last it did I got up and cleaned it up. Probably it was pointless to scold him. I'd adopted a fox, I'd have to figure out how to make that work. Or even anything at all.

CHAPTER THREE

I ALWAYS woke up feeling like the Creature from the Black Lagoon. I shambled to the toilet and then to the sink and then around the house a little to get used to it. By the time the coffee was done most of the seaweed had dropped off my brain.

I poured a bowl of Purina for my fox and freshened up his water, then got out my skillet. I laid out a couple of strips of bacon and pressed on the ends so they'd fry up even and not get all rubbery. I started a couple pieces of toast, the darkness set somewhere between 4 and 5. I melted some butter in a smaller pan and busted a couple of eggs in it and sprinkled them with fine black pepper out of a Sauer's tin.

I find the secret to good fried eggs is to open the shell close to the surface in a hot pan, and let the egg slip out gently so it doesn't splatter. Of course, I hate egg whites so I poked the yolks with the corner of the spatula and covered the pan with a lid so they'd cook evenly. When the toast popped I buttered it, flipped the two eggs onto it, broke my bacon strips in half, added them, and closed the sandwich. I drank a glass of juice and killed two cups of coffee. Then I tried walking the fox. We agreed never to attempt it again.

Once I'd showered and scrubbed my teeth I put on a pair of khakis and a denim shirt and drove to Dahlgren. I took the less direct route, through the courthouse area. The county seat might have been better placed at Office Hall or the Circle, but in the eighteenth century there'd been no bridges across the rivers to the north and south, and what eventually became route 3 was the only road that mattered. Now most of the traffic bypassed that stretch entirely.

The current courthouse was built in the early 20's in the neoclassical revival style, a broad, squat red-brick building with a columned portico, fanlights over the door and windows under the pediment. The street, though sleepy, still looked hopeful, without the sad air of a dead man's attic it eventually came to bear.

Across from the courthouse was a rather large store with a shining tin roof, a wide gallery facing Route 3 and a row of clock-face gas pumps in front. A large red porcelain-enameled sign above the porch steps said "NATION-WIDE SERVICE GROCERS," and painted on either side of the front door were the words "E.R. MORRIS AND SON."

I stopped in to pick up a paper and fill my gas tank. There was a Chevy dealer next door: a red-brick building that also bore the name Morris on the front. West of the Courthouse, most everything belonged either to the Morrises or the Clifts. Once you got past the Methodist and Episcopal churches, there was Clift's garage on the left, the Clift Motor Company on the right, a white cinder-block Ford dealer standing beside a cramped three-bay firehouse. Most of the firefighters were Clifts, too.

After that, it all sort of petered out. Dr. Arnold's house, Willow Hill, stood on the left just short of the intersection with Dahlgren Road, aptly called Arnold's Corner. On the right beyond the intersection was Arnold's Garage, a small clapboard filling station. I took the right onto Dahlgren Road, a narrow hilly route crowded by forest on both sides. There was no shoulder. There wasn't much other than a scattering of houses for most of the way.

I kept thinking about Miss Ethel. As I'd driven her home along the darkened, narrow path of Dahlgren Road the night before she said, "So. Cogbill. That ain't a local name, is it?"

"No ma'am." I kept scanning the edges of the forest for deer.

"You gonna tell me or do I have to guess?"

"Chesterfield," I said.

"South of Richmond. What brought you to King George?"

"Everywhere else was about used up."

"You don't want to tell me, that's fine."

"I had an army buddy from here."

"You look him up?"

"He didn't make it."

She didn't press further. My hands felt stiff on the wheel as the lights of the car kissed the treeline to either side of us. I thought of another forest far away, where better men than me had died and I had walked away, and I knew that I did not deserve Ethel Burkitt, or anyone else. Getting close would only hasten her departure from my life. What use would a strong, independent young woman have a for a broken-down old jackass whose main hobby was getting fired from things?

I was on the same road now, headed the other way, in the sunlight. I crossed Indian Town Road, and then the little Weedonville Post Office at my left on the corner of Hobson Lane, the color of goldenrod with a green roof, looking like it belonged on the set of a John Wayne movie with its crow steps and wide plank porch. An old white frame house with a tin roof and lightning rods sat out beyond the field next door.

The silvered carcass of a possum lay sprawled across the center of my lane, naked tail arrow-straight behind it. There was no gore; perhaps he was play-acting. I reckoned I knew how he felt. I straddled him with my tires as I passed.

Just beyond Weedonville there was a subdivision called Eden Estates under construction to the right. Just now this particular vision of Eden was a big swath of earth cut by bull-dozers through a mess of broken trees along Eden Drive. The name came from the estate that once stood on the property. In a county that was traditionally populated by farmers and wa-termen, a pocket of brick ramblers and cookie-cutter colonials would be a novelty; but the Navy had been in the county for about forty years, and the demand for housing had become impossible to ignore.

I passed the Cleydael estate, which was once the home of Dr. Richard Henry Stuart, and wondered if it might be the next piece of history to fall casualty to progress. John Wilkes Booth and David Herold had called upon the doctor seeking food, lodging, and medical attention in the days following Lin-coln's assassination. Stuart fed Booth and Herold, but did not permit them to stay.

Sometimes I wondered what it was like in the days be-fore our ancestors crossed the sea, when cinnamon-skinned warriors in moccasins and beaded leggings crept soundlessly through the shimmering forests, their chests and faces painted black and red, heads partially shaved, feathers and beads tied into raven-colored hair, jewelry of shell and bone strung from nose to ear. I don't know how that world sounded or smelled, but I am certain that it was full of magic and wonder, and I sometimes think they are still there, in the dark shapes that move through the periphery of my vision. Perhaps it is they of whom the trees whisper on autumn evenings when the shadows grow long and the first leaves begin to fall. Maybe everything that ever has or will exist is always there, beyond the fog, waiting to return.

The road dropped sharply downward, covered a short, narrow bridge across Peppermill Creek, and then angled steeply back uphill. A big pileated woodpecker flew across the road, bobbing up and down with the effort, the white under his wings flashing, his red crest swept back like a shark's fin. The trees were so close here that the branches met, high above the road, and blocked out most of the sun. Route 218 joined from the left at Berthaville, a colonial-era Episcopal church called St. Paul's set way back on the right, a huge, two-story block of brick, its footprint the shape of a Greek cross, hipped roof and plain glass windows. There was a big brick chimney, and no steeple.

The church had a kind of brooding symmetry, presiding over a yard of gnarled trees and ancient grave markers. It was an old place, and like many places I'd been in Europe, the air was heavy with the memory of the dead. The truth of human existence is that happiness comes only in short bursts to buoy us among the tragedy of loss and failures of the heart and the spirit. I needed a hit, and conjured Ethel's blue eyes and the sound of her voice, and saw the grasshoppers flying in from her father's field, her sun-gilded hair lifting in the breeze. Words tumbled out of her mouth like apples from an overturned basket, and her accent rang like barbed wire strung between log fence-posts topped with tin.

Then at last, I was in Owens, and near the corner of Windsor Drive was Owens Market, long and low, with a pent roof across the front and big display windows flanking the door. Beside it was an old whitewashed church with an open crawlspace, plain glass windows, tin roof, and an entryway with a fanlight over the door. The sign identified it as Oakland Baptist Church, and a small cemetery spread behind it and the Owens market.

I parked in the dust in front of the store. There was a guy in brown slacks and a rumpled grey blazer leaning on the fender of a black Caddy with Maryland tags. He had a yellow shirt and a striped tie, and a porkpie hat with a silk band in an ugly print. I recognized him as hat guy from Wilkerson's the night before. I hesitated a moment; I wondered if they knew Ethel, and if so would they remember me?

I got out of the car and headed for the store. As I passed the Caddy I nodded to the guy in the hat. "Nice day, innit?"

"Not so nice I don't wish I was anyplace else," he said. "What you guys do for fun around here? You got like, barn dances and stuff?"

"You're thinking of Oklahoma," I said. "This is Virginia. We mostly grow tobacco and write the Declaration of Independence."

"Hell," he said. "Guess somebody's got to."

The store had a familiar musty interior: worn hardwood floor, shelves stocked with basic groceries, hardware, housewares, and clothes. There was a tall dark-haired kid in an apron behind the counter.

"What's with the guy out front?" I said.

"His pals are in talking to Mr. Taylor."

At the name Taylor, my neck tightened up. My Army buddy's name was Taylor. I hoped to Christ I wasn't about to meet one of his relatives. I wasn't convinced they'd have anything to say to me, and I was even less convinced there was anything they'd want me to say to them.

"Mr. Taylor have a first name?"

"Yes sir, Mr. Bob Taylor."

I felt my shoulders come unwound.

"They from around here?"

"The Taylors?"

"The guys he's talking to."

"DC or Maryland I guess."

"They been in town long?"

"They been in here a couple times this week, I don't know. Maybe staying over at the Hillcrest or something."

"Could just as easily have driven down a couple of times this week."

"Sure. Like I said, I don't know."

"What's their business?"

"I'm not sure about that, either. They seem interested in land, but around here that's getting to be pretty reg'lar."

"They want to buy the store?"

"I don't know. They been in back a while."

I wandered down one of the aisles, feigning interest in a spinner rack full of signs that said things like "FOR SALE BY OWNER" and "BEWARE OF DOG." After a few minutes a door opened behind the counter and three men came out. One of them had greying hair parted to the left and draped across his forehead, and a cowlick. He was wearing a white apron and khaki trousers, and a short-sleeved button-down shirt; obviously Mr. Taylor, and for sure no relation of Rollie's.

The other two were familiar. I'd seen them in Wilkerson's the night before. One guy was sort of narrow, with a white shirt and a painted necktie, black pants and a grey blazer. His hair was curly and swept back from his forehead. The other was shorter and heavier, and dressed a little better than either his companion or the guy leaning on the car out front. He had a gold wristwatch and a ring on his right hand.

He put his hand on Taylor's shoulder, said something softly and shook his hand. Then he patted him once on the back, and he and his companion cruised on out the door, got in the Caddy and drove away towards Dahlgren. Taylor turned and regarded me, and sent his helper off to sweep the store.

"What can I do for you today?"

"You don't have any signs say BEWARE OF FOX, do you?"

Taylor laughed hesitantly. "Ah, no, don't reckon I do. That's a new one. Having fox problems?"

"Well, there's one in my house."

Taylor opened his mouth and then closed it again.

"Who were those guys, anyway? They don't look like they're from around here."

"Just passing through," Taylor said. "Needed directions."

"Where to?"

"Richmond."

"Went the wrong way, didn't they?"

"City folk, you know how it is."

"Yeah, reckon I do. Say, you know the guy owns that air strip up yonder off 301?"

"That'll be Jack Pope. Well, Jack and his mother, since Jim passed."

"He give flying lessons?"

"Jack? He did, reckon he may still."

"Thanks. What did Jim die of?"

"Jim who?"

"Jim Pope, I assume."

There was a long, awkward moment while Taylor and I stared at each other.

"Does it matter?"

"To somebody, I hope."

"What'd you say your name was, sir?"

"Cogbill. Harry."

"You ain't from around here yourself, or I'd know you."

"I live out near Gera, but I thought I might take up flying."

"Almost be closer go out to Oak Grove, wouldn't it? They got that big fancy airport for the beach. Bet some fellow out there would teach you."

"It was recommended I talk to Mr. Pope."

I was getting a funny read off Taylor.

"You alright, Mr. Taylor? You seem nervous. Those guys didn't threaten you, did they?"

"Lord, no. You're an inquisitive fellow, ain't you?"

"Well, you know what they say."

"What's that?"

"I don't know, I was asking you."

A slow grin spread across Taylor's face.

"You're a real piece of work, Mr. Cogbill."

"I've been told."

"Well if you don't mind, I got to take inventory here."

"Sure."

"Be careful at that intersection, now. Watch out for trucks coming down the hill. They won't see you until it's too late, you know they cain't stop on a dime."

"Thanks, I'll be careful."

"Been a lot of deaths on the highway," he said. "Some new family every week. Real shame."

I did not get killed pulling out onto Highway 301. Jack Pope's service station was only about a mile north, standing at the entrance to the air field. It had a gravel turnaround and a couple of modern pumps with fluorescent lights like wings spread protectively above. There were two buildings: a modern cinder block structure with a couple of bays that had an office and a waiting area; and a green clapboard building with a tin gambrel roof, wedged on an awkward little plot behind the filling station, partially hidden from the highway by a line of cedar trees.

There was a bright yellow J-3 Piper Cub out on the grass near the runway. I could see way back across the low, grass-covered airfield to what looked like a fence and a ragged treeline, and a ridge beyond that climbed higher to the south, toward Cloverdale house. A culvert ran across the airfield, from the direction of Williams Creek, under the main runway, which ran sort of southeast to northwest. The whole field was shaped something like a boot. Ethel had told me there was another runway, along the back edge of the property running northeast-southwest.

I stepped up and through the office door on the right front of the gas station.

"Owner around?"

"That's me," said a tall, narrow guy with wavy hair in light brown going grey. "Jack Pope."

"I just helped some guys change a flat back there on 206," I said. "They forgot their tire iron. They mentioned having just been here. Bad timing and all that. They headed back this way and I thought they might have come by for a patch or something, maybe I could catch them."

"Nobody's been in for a patch," Jack said. "But if they're locals I probably know them. Did you get their names?"

"No sir, I didn't. It was three guys in a black Cadillac."

Jack's face changed, but only briefly.

"They said they stopped here?"

"That was the impression I got."

"I think I'd recall a Caddy," he said.

"Well, it was worth a shot."

"Look, I could be wrong, I see a lot of cars. If you want to leave the lug wrench with me, I'll see they get it, if they show up."

"That your airfield out there?"

There was the dull thump of an explosion in the distance behind me as a bunch of scientists and Navy guys over on the base fired the guns out on the main range. An image of blood-spattered snow flashed before my eyes. I swallowed my nerves as the concussion wave rattled through the shop.

"Don't worry about that," Pope said. "Just your tax dollars at work."

"I've been thinking of learning to fly. I don't know why, I guess being forty is kind of tough to get a handle on."

"Well sir, I've been known to give a lesson or two, but the truth is I just sold the whole thing. I'm going to have to move my plane, maybe to Shannon or someplace, and I'm afraid it's just a lousy piece of timing."

"It can't stay here?"

"Not gonna be an airfield anymore."

"Well that's a damn shame. It have something to do with the base?"

Jack Pope looked at me sort of funny again.

"No. Why would you mention the base?"

"Well, there could have been some conflict."

"What did you say your name was?"

"Cogbill. I say something wrong?"

"I'm just not sure I like your tone, sir."

"I believe you may have misunderstood me, Mr. Pope."

"I wouldn't rule it out. Like you said, age is tough to get a handle on."

I couldn't see much benefit to roughing him up, and I didn't think I could scare the hell out of anyone, so I left. I drove north on 301, past Wilkerson's. No Cadillac was there. I turned off at the wayside by the Morgantown Bridge, a small river beach with a public boat ramp. I turned the car around and headed back south, then made a left onto B-Gate road and drove in to Dahlgren proper.

There were a few bungalows along the right-hand side and a chain-link fence topped with barbed wire and posted with government warning signs at regular intervals along the left. Just before the road intersected with route 206, I could see the end of the navy runway, this one blacktopped and well-marked, and then the fence turned at 90 degrees away from me and cut across a field. On the right side of the intersection was Potomac Elementary School, a new flat-roofed job with broad windows across the front and a gravel turnaround. On the opposite corner was a cinderblock Shell station.

I made a shallow left turn onto 206 toward the Main Gate of the NWL. Just before the gate – which was really just a little brick booth with a gabled roof – was a turnoff on the right and a big brick building with dentils and a columned portico, a broad circle in front with three flagpoles, a blue US Mail drop, and a huge grey naval anchor: the Dahlgren Post Office. Federal bureaucracy in action – put the guards in a shoebox and the bills in a palace. It was a long shot, and there was no Caddy there, either. I watched a large grocery truck get checked in at the gate, maybe heading for the commissary or the PX.

I pulled back out onto 206 and drove west, away from the gate, towards 301. I could kill an entire day and several tanks of gas doing this, but to what end? I wondered what a detective would do. Somebody ought to hire one. Out at the main intersection I eased onto 301 South and climbed the hill.

There at the summit, on the left-hand side, was the Hillcrest Motel, long and low, with a ridiculous array of weather vanes. Next to it stood the matching brick diner with a gabled roof and green awnings. Beyond and a little behind this was a swimming pool. Parked in front of the Motel was a black Cadillac. Well, there was no getting around it. Now I had to do something. Maybe surveil. That seemed like the professional thing.

I pulled in and parked in front of the diner. What the hell, what was the worst that could happen? A fish crow started awping in the trees behind the motel. In hindsight, he probably knew something I didn't.

CHAPTER FOUR

I TUCKED the newspaper under my arm, climbed a couple of brick steps and pressed the brass thumb-latch on the entry door. Inside the Hillcrest Grill was paneled in pine from floor to ceiling. There was a big wood counter at the back of the room and a pair of swinging doors into the kitchen. Booths lined the walls and several tables stood in the middle of the room.

Each booth had an electric wall sconce at about shoulder height for the diners, patterned after colonial tin candle sconces with reflector plates. The electric candles had special flame-tipped bulbs that burned with a dim orange glow and alternated current through two or three different filaments to create the illusion of a flickering flame. Rustic. It was a little early for lunch and the place was almost empty.

I picked a booth near the corner, by the only window from which I could see the hotel, and when the waitress came with a glass of water I ordered coffee, and a burger with fries. I sent the cream and sugar back.

The King George News was published on Thursdays. The front page, as it did almost every week, had a photo of the mangled wreck of a car and a story about some family who had been killed on 301; either in King George, or a King George family who had been traveling through Caroline County. Other than that, what passed for reporting was mostly thin coverage of local events, a calendar of Church meetings and a list of who had gone visiting family or friends in other states. The Circle Market had paid for a two-page ad.

I was still waiting on the burger when I saw the three guys come out of a room halfway down the motel. If I had to bail on my food I was going to be disappointed. But they bypassed the caddy and headed for the diner. I made it a point not to look when they walked in the door and headed for the back corner. The waitress brought them menus and glasses of water.

I sipped my coffee and studied an advertisement for brassieres. I wondered briefly how uncomfortable they were. The illustrator who drew the ad had rendered an attractive, slender blonde who looked pretty thrilled about the one she was wearing. Advertisements were always full of drawings of women who were way too happy about crummy things like vacuum cleaners and soap.

I imagined Ethel would have something witty to say about that, and I caught myself smiling, which made it awkward when the waitress brought me my burger and glanced at the page I had open. I thanked her and smiled politely, and she gave me a look that suggested I probably should get out more, but she was too interested in her tip to say so.

As I turned the page, I glanced up and saw one of the three men at the table looking at me. It was the curly-haired one, and it was not a friendly look. Perhaps he needed a new vacuum cleaner. Or one of the bras like the lady in the picture. I knocked some ketchup out of the glass bottle and onto the edge of my plate, twisted the cap back on and started on my fries.

Mr. and Mrs. Clarence Tunney had gone visiting Mrs. Tunney's parents in Schenectady. Someone named Lucy Payne had recently come home visiting from Radford. Move over, Ed Murrow. I glanced up again, and now two of the guys were looking at me: Curly and The Hat. Hat had to look over his shoulder to do it. Stocky was sitting with his back to the wall, but he was busy adding cream and sugar to his coffee. Infidel.

The high school had a column called "The Fox's Howl," but I didn't read it. I was too busy running over the two previous times I'd seen the three men in the Cadillac, and wondering if they had any particular reason to be suspicious of me, apart from the frequency of our encounters. I decided they probably wouldn't threaten me. Not yet. It would only make it obvious that they had something to hide, and if they were the kind of guys I thought they were, they would be more careful than that. They were letting me know I had their attention.

The Volunteer Firemen's sandlot ball team had won in extra innings. I finished my meal and got up to pay my tab at the counter, and The Hat went outside. Maybe I was mistaken about how careful they were. I popped a toothpick out of a dispenser, left a tip on the table, and stuck the King George News back under my arm. It had about as many pages as a tabloid. Curly watched me walk out. Stocky was reading the Washington Post. He probably didn't know about the firemen.

As I stepped down to the asphalt, I saw The Hat leaning on the fender of my car.

"Yo, I'd say we didn't recognize this crate a yours when we was walking over here, but it's actually pretty tough to forget, what with being such a piece a shit an' all."

"Man, I'll bet you work at the Pickle Factory," I said.

"What the fuck is a pickle factory?"

"Where they make pickles."

"Okay, Milton Berle. Everybody knows them grows on trees."

"I'll be sure to put that in the Declaration of Independence."

He looked at me with a dead stare. I was not sure if he understood that I was insulting him. I had not given him enough credit, but in my defense I did not at the time understand the kind of man he was.

"Hope y'all are enjoying your visit," I said. "But if you don't mind, I need to go buy a vacuum cleaner, or possibly some soap."

"No problem," he said. "Mister Vasiliou and Mister Drakos was just wondering if you needed any help. See we get that it's not a very big town you has here, and we keep bumping into you, like neighbors, but everybody has been so accommodating that Mister Vasiliou just thought maybe he could return the favor."

"Well, you're the guests here, all you need to do is make yourselves at home, I'm sure."

"I had to check, is all. See Mister Vasiliou and Mister Drakos hates it when people get into trouble. That ain't the kind of thing they can bear to see. You understand?"

"Humanitarians. I was really just hoping to take some flying lessons, but it seems the Popes are closing up their airfield."

"I heard."

"It's kind of strange, don't you think, what with Jack Pope being a pilot and all?"

"Things change."

"When in the course of human events it becomes necessary," I said.

"Be careful driving," he said. "This hill is dangerous."

"Right."

"Take it easy, Mister Cogbill." He turned and walked away.

"I don't recall telling you my name," I said.

He skipped one of the front steps, with his long stride, and disappeared through the white door of the diner.

I stood there for a while, various scenarios of increasing horror playing out in my head. They knew who I was, and they'd seen me with Ethel in Wilkerson's last night. Although it was August I was freezing cold, remembering how blood steamed on clean white snow. I drove back to Owens market before I even realized I had done it, taking Windsor drive from 301, coming out next to Oakland Baptist on 206.

Taylor's assistant was out front, hosing down the turnaround in front of the store. When I went inside, Mr. Taylor was there reading the paper and drinking a Royal Crown Cola. I knocked the RC out of his hand, the bottle landing on the hardwood with a thump, the brown cola running between the boards.

"Hey, what in God's name are you doing?!"

I grabbed him by his belt and his apron straps and pitched him through the door into the back room. I went in after him and locked the door. I couldn't breathe. My hands were shaking and all I could think about was the sun in Ethel's hair, but it wasn't calming me down, it was winding me up. My chest was tightening and my breath came in short rasps. My neck was pulsing, and I could barely hear Taylor's voice over the sound of the blood in my veins, like a trash bag full of wet rags being rolled down a flight of stairs.

"Mister Cogbill please, I didn't have no choice."

"Sit down."

"You don't know who these men are, I didn't have no choice."

"SIT THE GODDAMNED HELL DOWN." I needn't have said it; for as I did, I shoved him in the chest like a kicking mule, and he went down into the chair and the chair tipped over and slammed him against a metal filing cabinet behind him. I believe a drawer handle caught him on the back of the head.

"Sir you can beat on me all you want and it ain't bad as what them men will do."

"Who are they?"

"Businessmen from Baltimore, or DC I cain't keep it straight."

"Bullshit."

"That's who they are, they're buying up land for development. That's all."

"Then why are you so terrified of them?"

"Why are you? You ain't come in here laying about with threats because they impressed you with their kindness."

"You were lying to me this morning sir, and you're lying to me now."

The kid started knocking on the door.

"Mister Taylor, is ever'thing all right?"

My breathing had started to level out, and the wet rags had slowed their descent. I leaned down until my face was an inch from Taylor's.

"If anything happens to her I will beat you until whatever's left runs between these floor boards. On my honor, Taylor."

He swallowed, and nodded once.

He called out in his nearest approximation of good cheer, "Joe, everything's fine in here. Mr. Cogbill and I's just discussing a line of credit."

I opened the door and damn near knocked the kid over. My left shoe accidentally caught the RC bottle and sent it spinning across the floor.

I heard Taylor say, "well don't just stand there Joe, get a mop for God's sake," and then the front door swung shut behind me and I peeled out of the lot and headed for the Burkitt place.

I was not driving at a safe or reasonable rate of speed. The lack of a shoulder on 206 probably saved me; the sheriff and the state police didn't patrol it because there was nowhere to pull anyone over. I had a near-miss in Berthaville with a convertible coming off 218. At Weedonville, three dark shapes hunched over the dead possum: one black vulture and two turkey buzzards, red ribbons of rent flesh littering the pavement in a macabre starburst and glistening on the featherless faces of the scavengers. Intent on their work, they barely registered my passage.

By the time I hit Indian Town Road I could just about hear the blood in my veins over the sound of the engine. I took the left on Indian Town, cutting off Arnold's Corner and coming out on Route 3 by Clift's Garage, then right past the Clift Motor Company and a left by St. Anthony's onto Millbank Road, back past the school and out into open country.

I took the Burkitt driveway so fast I thought I was going to bust the Hudson's crankshaft on every bump I hit. The springs screamed and the frame groaned and one of my hub-caps popped off with a loud "ronk", skipped with a clang in the orange dirt, leaped ten feet over the barbed-wire and rolled away across the field.

I skidded to a halt, left my car door standing open and raced around the back of the house toward the chicken coop. She wasn't there. I rushed into the barn and nearly caught a pitchfork with my face.

"Sweet Lord, Cogbill, that was a close—"

She didn't finish her sentence because I scooped her up in my arms and kissed her so hard I thought we may have been legally married. She kissed me back and put her hands in my hair and then her father walked in with my hubcap in his hands and said, "son what in the hell is the matter with you?"

I set his daughter back on her feet and she wheeled on him. "Daddy Franklin Burkitt that is no way to talk to a guest."

"Well you sure to hell gave him a warm welcome." He spat tobacco juice in the dirt and the straw.

"And for God's sake can you not do that in here? It's disgusting."

"It's a barn, pumpkin, animals shit in here."

"That is true, but the last I checked none of them chewed tobacco."

Mr. Burkitt pressed the hubcap into my chest until I took hold of it.

"Next time you roll one of these across my field, son, you'll be wearing it as a hat."

He stormed out of the barn.

"I messed up," I said.

"He's just worried I might run away with you, Cogbill, and leave him to run this place all by himself."

"You might be in danger."

"If one of us is in danger from my daddy it ain't me, sir."

"You're not listening to me. I messed up today and you might be in danger. I think it's time we called the Sheriff."

"Wait, start at the beginning."

"Jack Pope's your uncle, right?"

"Yes, my mother was his sister."

"How did your grandfather, Jim, die?"

"Heart attack."

"That what the coroner said?"

"Oh for God's sake, he died and they put him in a box and buried him, who needs all that other business?"

"No coroner?"

"No, why does that matter?"

"Did you see the body?"

"No, but Uncle Jack did and that's good enough ain't it? What's this about?"

"I spent the day driving around Owens and Dahlgren and getting lied to by everybody I met. Including Mr. Taylor at the Owens market. Including your Uncle Jack. And then those guys from Wilkerson's last night threatened me, and they know my name, and based on what they said they got it from Taylor, and they saw you with me in Wilkerson's, and if I keep pushing this they might hurt you."

"Harry Cogbill if they even set foot on this farm we will shoot them to death and that'll be the end of it."

"Maybe."

"What do you mean, maybe?"

"The guy who threatened me. He said 'yo'."

"What the hell's that mean?"

"It's a greeting. 'Yo, gimme one wit'.' It's a Philadelphia thing."

"Aren't we a little beyond worrying about Northern aggression, Cogbill?"

"They're Greeks. I don't know The Hat's name but the other two are Vasiliou and Drakos. There's a Greek Mafia operates out of Philly and Baltimore. I think our friends might have connections. I think they might have bought your Uncle's air field. I don't know why."

"And with that you want to go to the Sheriff?"

She was right. It was thin. It would get me laughed out of the courthouse.

"Let's go to Fredericksburg tonight. You and me. We'll get dinner someplace nice, we'll go see a movie."

"You're running away."

"I'm trying to protect you."

"I can take care of myself."

"I know you can."

"That why you came barreling down the driveway so hard you lost a hubcap, damn near lost your face on a pitchfork and give me a kiss like you ain't seen me in ten years?"

"I have felt more alive in the last thirty-six hours than I have in twenty years, Miss Ethel. I respect your strength. You make me better. How could I ever bear to lose that?"

"Why would you have to?"

I couldn't decide how to answer.

"Hrmm? What's wrong with you, Harry Cogbill? No that's not an insult, it's a genuine question, something is bothering you and it ain't just some northern thugs."

"It's me, I'm just...I don't know."

"You respect my strength, how about trusting me, too?"

"Yes ma'am. Reckon I can do that."

"Come see me tomorrow and we'll talk. I don't think it's a good idea to go out tonight."

"Why not?"

"Because you look a little wild and you ain't being straight with me, and I frankly am not in the mood."

"I understand."

She walked me to my car. I threw the hubcap in the backseat and we kissed goodbye. I was coming down off the anger and the panic, and even kissing Miss Ethel hadn't made the sun come out inside of me. I should have been ecstatic that she was talking about trust, but she was cross with me and I knew from this point on every decision I made would only make it worse, and I had no idea how to stop the plane from crashing into the sea. Whatever was wrong with me was in the driver's seat now.

I drove back to Millbank Road and out to Route 3 at Saint Anthony's and the school, and I turned right to head east toward the courthouse. I parked on the street and walked in the front door. One long central hallway ran the width of the building, and at the east end was a vault door, where you stepped up into the Clerk of Court's Office. The Clerk was named Lawrence Mason, and he'd held the office since 1917.

I located the most recent deed book, a big, heavy white tome that slid on rollers out of a metal shelving unit, and laid it out on the angled workspace atop the storage unit. I went to the last page and worked my way back, looking for the deed to the Pope land. If the sale was recent it would be on record.

Early on I found a deed of trust signed between Dimitrios Vasiliou and Sophia Vasiliou, parties of the first part, and Nikolaos Drakos, party of the second part, transferring ownership of all that land in the Potomac Magisterial District, consisting of 161.57 acres, more or less, being the same land conveyed by J. A. Pope and Vashti S. Pope to Dimitrios and Sophia Vasiliou in October of 1956. Witnessed and signed by Lawrence Mason.

There was a handwritten marginal note referring to another deed, and after following the marginal notes from deed to deed for a few hours, I learned that when James Pope died in 1956 the land had passed to his widow, Vashti, and their son, Jack; and that the two of them had conveyed part of the land to a couple from New York, whose names I did not recognize, and then conveyed the rest to Vasiliou and his wife in 1957, who in turn had signed it over to a developer called Marsden Homes, whose vice-president was Nikolaos Drakos, and whose secretary was Dimitrios Vasiliou himself. Likewise a second organization, run by someone named Hector Adagio and L. Thomas Boone, had acquired the land from the New York couple and deeded it to Marsden Homes. The whole thing felt shady.

Still, none of these conveyances and liens, in the amount of thirty-two thousand dollars, amounted to anything illegal or Mason couldn't have affixed his seal to them. Which meant the real question was what in the hell was going on out at Pope's Field, and for how long? I'd need some evidence before I could go to the Sheriff. I drove across the street, topped off the gas tank at the Morris's, and bought a Coke. Then I drove to Gera and borrowed John's phone at the store.

Len Mahoney, the one cop I knew back in Boston, was happy to talk to me until I told him I needed a favor. Then he said, "Christ, Cogbill, I thought we was friends." He drove a streamroller over all his vowel sounds when he said it.

"Len, I might be in real trouble here. All I'm asking for is some background."

"When the hell did you become a private eye?"

"This morning. Well, yesterday afternoon. I mean I'm not really a PI."

"Stop talking. I mean it, I don't want to hear another word."

"Look if you won't do it I know a guy manages a casino who might be able to get me what I need, but we didn't exactly part on the best terms, and—"

"Stop it. Stop talking. I'm hanging up now."

"Len, there are lives at stake. There may have been a murder."

"Not in my jurisdiction."

"Because lives in Boston matter more."

"They do to me."

"Bullshit."

"What is it exactly you're asking for?"

I told him the names Dimitrios Vasiliou and Nikolaos Drakos. I threw in Hector Adagio and L. Thomas Boone as a bonus. Gave him the number at the store, told him he could leave the information with John. Then I told John to take careful notes when Len called him back, and not to tell a soul.

"You know I wouldn't go gossiping nobody's business around the county, Mr. Cogbill."

"Right. That's why I'm helping Miss Ethel with this thing."

"Ya'll got a date out of it too, din'tcha?"

"John..."

"I cain't help if people tell me things."

By now it was getting late. I went home and cleaned up the mess the fox had made while I was gone. When I was done I made a grilled cheese and a can of soup and a pot of coffee. This pet fox business was not going well. The furniture was trashed, I kept finding poop in weird places and being a grey fox he liked to climb things. I was going to need to build him an outdoor enclosure and a doghouse, and maybe put in a doggie door.

"I should have got a cat," I said. The fox just grinned at me.

As long as I was reviewing my errors in judgment, I shouldn't have made coffee. I should have gone to bed. But that would only hasten tomorrow, and I was not ready for that. I finished my dinner and sat there in the kitchen under the fluorescent nautilus, dirty dishes in front of me, pots and pans piled in the sink, listening to insects singing through my open window, my thoughts like squid's ink rolling behind my eyes. The fox jumped onto the kitchen table, looked expectantly at me for a moment, and then began licking my empty soup bowl.

"Yep. I guess I've pretty much ruined everything."

CHAPTER FIVE

BY THE TIME I fell asleep the sun was starting to come up, but my funk had only deepened. I woke to the sound of someone banging on my front door. I staggered around like Frankenstein's monster and somehow managed to get pants on. I was pulling my shirt on when I got to the door and found Ethel Burkitt on my porch. I squinted at the sun out beyond the railing. Ethel looked disappointed, and I thought I could feel her judging me, but the truth is when I am in one of my moods I cannot be depended upon to reliably read a room.

"Lord, Cogbill, did you tie one on last night or what?"

"I don't drink."

"You got company?"

"What? No...I don't do that, either. I mean, not...not with...no."

"May I come in?"

"Yeah, of course." I stepped back and let her in.

I buttoned my shirt and tucked it in, as well as I could before coffee, anyway, and then fumbled around with the tin percolator.

"You sure you don't drink?"

"Not good at mornings."

"It's past lunchtime."

"Not good at waking up," I said, swearing as I spilled coffee grounds all over the Formica.

"Let me help you."

"For Christ's sake, Ethel, I can make coffee."

"Well, you finally put a sentence together, that's a start."

Eventually I got the percolator assembled and the coffee started.

"I'm sorry about yesterday," I said.

Ethel nodded.

"It's all right, Cogbill."

"No, it's not."

"I didn't come here to beat you up, so stop doing it preemptively."

"Sure. Okay."

The afternoon sun streamed in rays through the window and fell in bars across Ethel's chest. She stood there with her arms folded, weight settled on one hip. The percolator sighed and burbled rhythmically. I was leaning on my kitchen counter and she stood across from me in the relatively small space.

She'd been hard at work on the farm and her scent was musky and slightly sour, and the truth is I didn't mind. Today Ethel's overalls were newer and fit her a little better, and the plaid shirt was green and blue, and it went well with her coloring. I considered saying so, but I wasn't sure how much trouble I was in and I decided to hold my tongue.

"I feel like I forced you into this, Cogbill. If you don't want to investigate, if this isn't something you want to do, then don't. It's okay with me. You can keep the money, too. But don't for God's sake start avoiding me."

"You think I'm doing this because I'm desperate for money?"

"It had crossed my mind."

"Ethel."

"But after the way you were carrying on yesterday I know that's not the case."

"I was out of control."

"Yes you were."

"I've failed at a lot of things in my life."

"Oh cut that out. 'I've failed at a lot of things,' who hasn't, Harry Cogbill?"

"What I mean to say is, if this private eye thing goes all sideways I don't want to take you down with me."

The color of her eyes was electric as she looked up at me and twisted her mouth off to one side.

"Hieronymus will you by God stop worrying everything to death."

"I just mean that I care about you."

"You know what your problem is?"

"I have a feeling you're about to tell me."

"You're afraid of being happy."

"What kind of damn fool thing to say is that?"

"The true kind. I don't know what you think you need to atone for, but I ain't a preacher and Lord knows I ain't no angel. I run my mouth a little too much but the only kind of bullshit I'll put up with is what we spread in the field."

"I'm sorry, Ethel."

"Am I standing here right now? Are we together?"

"Together?"

"If your head was any harder you'd have a great career in demolition."

"You're an exceptional lady, Ethel."

"Well that'll do. Now are you going to offer me a cup of coffee and tell me what the hell happened yesterday, or am I going home?"

"Ethel."

"I know I'm all dirty and sweaty and I ain't all prettied up. It's okay, I understand."

"Ethel, you're beautiful."

"Let's not go crazy, Cogbill."

I thought it was possible I already had.

"Have you had lunch, Ethel?"

"I have not."

"Well, let me fix you some."

"I don't mind breakfast for lunch."

"At this hour? I'll fix a proper lunch."

I had some sliced honey ham and some swiss cheese in the ice box, and half a loaf of rye in the breadbox. I did up some bacon in the skillet, careful not to leave it in too long, and then set that aside and made ham and swiss sandwiches on rye and added the bacon, then grilled the sandwiches lightly so the cheese would soften up. While that was going I tossed a small salad with some leaf lettuce, tomatoes, and red onions. I didn't really like salad but I thought she might. I didn't have any dressing but I got out some oil and vinegar.

Probably awakened by the smell of the food, my fox had ventured out from under my bed to see what was going on, and Ethel held him in her lap and stroked his fuzzy cheeks and told him he was precious.

"He may poop on you," I said.

"Well, we'll need to work on that."

I plated up the sandwiches and poured us some coffee and we ate on the porch, rocking side by side, and she listened intently, her eyes on me as I recounted the previous day's mis-adventures.

"Why would Uncle Jack lie to you?"

"Well, I can think of some reasons."

"He ain't the type to get mixed up with those dirtbags. And he sure as hell wouldn't sell out the airfield, he loves flying too much."

"You know him better than I do," I said.

"Why did you ask how Grandpa Jim died?"

"Just a feeling. After I left your place yesterday afternoon I went to the courthouse and looked through the deeds in the Clerk's office. Vasiliou and Drakos have been in the mix for at least three years. Jim died in '56, right?"

"In mid-August, yes."

The hairs on the back of my neck felt like iron filings under a magnet's pull.

"Ethel do you remember when he bought that piece of land?"

"Not clearly, I was just a little girl. Cain't have been much later than '42."

"It was 1941, Ethel. August 17th, 1941. What was the exact date of his death?"

"Oh hell I don't know, who remembers a thing like that? You can find out for yourself you know, his grave is in the family plot just off the side of the highway, before you get to the creek. What's all this about, Cogbill? What am I not seeing?"

"Maybe nothing. Could be any of a dozen varieties of nothing. Your uncle did seem sad about closing the airfield. Maybe he didn't have a choice."

"Lot of developers buying up old land around here."

"Good money in real estate."

"Selling off old farmland ain't illegal, Cogbill, even if I'd like it to be."

"No," I agreed. "It's not. But murder sure is."

After we ate I rinsed off the plates and she volunteered to help with the dishes. I wasn't planning to do them anytime soon, but I liked having her around, so I washed and she dried and we talked about our families and our histories. Strange how I could crawl into bed one morning feeling like a leper and wake up in the afternoon like Lazarus from the grave.

"Ride with me over to the store so I can check my mail. I'm waiting for a phone call, too. It pertains to the case."

"Thank you for lunch. I'd better get back home before my daddy has himself a conniption fit. Come get me at six o'clock and you can take me bowling in town, Harry Cogbill. I don't like movie dates, nobody can talk to each other."

"I'll sure be glad to take you anywhere you like, Miss Ethel. But ride with me to the post office."

"You know that's gonna set John to talking."

"John's already talking."

We each picked up our mail. Len hadn't called me back, yet. John assured me he remembered, and that he'd take careful notes. I bought a prybar and a Free Lance-Star. He never stopped smiling at us.

"Sometimes I'd like to knock that guy out," I said as I drove away.

"He's good people."

"Didn't say he wasn't. But all the same."

Ethel smiled and shook her head.

"You're not the type."

I thought of Taylor out at the Owens store, and felt a sense of shame so overpowering that I had to hold Ethel's hand and feel the reassuring press of her slender fingers before I could respond.

"You're probably right."

Back at my house, we exchanged car keys, kissed good-bye, and she drove away in my Hudson. It was her suggestion: the hoods up at Owens knew my car, when I told her what I had planned she felt I'd be safer if I had a different vehicle.

"Ethel, don't they know your truck?"

"I doubt it. Besides, there's nowhere safer than home. We're armed and we can see them coming long before they get anywhere near us. Will you just take the truck and quit arguing with me?"

"Yes ma'am."

I still hated it, but the way I saw it I had only two ways forward. I had to either find something incriminating against Vasiliou and his crew, or I had to wring the truth out of Ethel's uncle Jack. Given my relationship to Ethel, one of these was distinctly preferable to the other.

I showered and shaved and put on a pair of olive-colored work pants and a khaki shirt, and screwed my fedora down low on my head. I got an old pair of Army field glasses down from the closet and put them, the prybar, and the newspaper in the truck. I took 205 to the traffic circle, and then 301 North back toward Dahlgren, and the realm of Messrs. Vasiliou, Drakos, and The Philadelphia Hat.

It was late summer, mid-afternoon and though the shadows were lengthening, fall was not yet in the air. The old Ford chugged along highway 301, the throttle a little loose, the clutch a little less responsive than I was accustomed to in my

Hornet. The flattened bugs on the windshield were catching the sun in the silhouette of the place cleared by the wipers in the last rainfall.

The radio was tuned to a country station and I let it play, Patsy Cline singing "Walkin' After Midnight" over a walking bassline and a crying steel guitar. She would re-record that one several times, but the 1957 version was always my favorite.

Patsy – born Virginia Patterson Hensley – was from Frederick County, Virginia, just outside Winchester, a community called Gore where the author Willa Cather was born. Frederick County is a beautiful, if somewhat remote area of the Shenandoah Valley, near the northernmost point of the state, nestled in the crook of West Virginia's broken thumb. Patsy's voice carried both the sultriness of a cabaret jazz singer and the frankness of a country girl, and if there has ever been a better singer I have yet to hear her.

When I got to the Hillcrest, I pulled around past the diner and parked way back in the lot, near the swimming pool. There were several cars and probably fifty or sixty yards between me and the Cadillac. I got out the Free Lance and tried to read about whatever people were concerned with in Fredericksburg, but it turned out I didn't care.

I checked out the sports page; Harmon Killibrew was still tearing it up for the Senators, but it was almost a waste. They might finally be shaping up but everyone knew Calvin Griffith was planning to move the team to Minneapolis. The Orioles were closing out their fifth season in Baltimore and though they weren't contenders that year, it was clear they were on their way up; and their third baseman, Brooks Robinson, was almost superhuman. Football season was barely starting, but Johnny Unitas and the Baltimore Colts were poised to have a big year, and although I liked Eddie LeBaron I doubted the Redskins had much of a season ahead of them.

I dug out the comics page to see what Charlie Brown was up to when Vasiliou, Drakos and The Hat got in their car and headed north. I figured I had a little while to look around. Now, what I was about to do was illegal, but I was already investigating without a license so I might as well jump in and get wet all at once.

I walked around behind the motel, to the bathroom window, and used my new prybar to wreck the Hillcrest's window locks. The bathroom had a tile floor and narrow little tub. There was a porcelain pedestal sink with white cross handles. There was a shaving kit on a little shelf. All the towels were hung up neatly, which I guess said something about whichever one of them used this room.

Through the narrow wooden door was the bedroom. It matched the interior of the diner, wood paneled from ceiling to floor, with a heavy curtain across the front window and a coat rack across the back of the door. There was a leather suitcase on the dresser. The nameplate on it said DIMITRIOS VASILIOU. Nothing in it but shirts, socks, and underwear. An extra pair of trousers. Judging by the wardrobe, Vasiliou was the short, stocky one, which meant the narrow, curly-headed fellow was probably Drakos.

I don't know what I expected to find. A diagram of their nefarious plan and a statement of murderous intent would have been a good start. Maybe a bunch of knives and guns and spare bullets. As it turned out he hadn't packed any of that, but he did have a couple of neckties, one with stripes and one with a pattern that looked like a rain of little silk hankies. The guy was orderly. Like the towels in the bathroom. A place for everything. And he was packed for maybe a week but he was living out of his suitcase. Not a motel unpacker. I respected that. There's something a little not right about a motel unpacker.

I dumped out his wastebasket and pawed through it. A few receipts from local businesses, the packaging for some shoelaces, the cellophane off a pack of cigarettes. A strand of dental floss. Nothing scandalous at all. Not so much as a used rubber. I chucked the garbage back in the little wastebasket, put the basket back where it belonged. On a whim I checked under the mattress. Nothing there, either. Dresser drawers empty except a Gideon Bible and a buffalo nickel. I kept the nickel. Finally I gave it up and climbed back out the bathroom window.

The second room was only a little more enlightening than the first. It was the mirror image, except nothing was particularly neat. The towels were sloppy, one was on the floor. There was a toothbrush encrusted with orange dirt chucked among the floss and the soap-wrappers in the bathroom wastebasket. I couldn't imagine what had caused such grievous condition in a toothbrush.

In the bedroom, both beds had been used and there were two suitcases, one neatly stowed and belted shut, the other standing partially open with various haberdashery spilling out of it. There were two more shoelace packages in the bedroom trashcan, just like in Vasiliou's room.

The messy suitcase held nothing of interest. The neat one had a box of .22 caliber bullets and a kit for cleaning a gun, down among the rolled-up boxer shorts and sock garters. Somebody was a pro. I guessed the Hat. I tucked everything back the way I found it, and got out of there.

The sun was going down and the cicadas, crickets, and katydids were singing in the trees. It was possibly my favorite sound in the world. I was almost back to the truck when a man came out of the office and asked if he could help me.

"Checking the meter," I said. What meter that would be I couldn't have told him, but it confused him long enough for me to get in the truck and drive off with only one minor hiccup on the clutch.

I drove down the hill and took the right on 206 toward the base, then left in front of Potomac Elementary and past the runway and the bungalows and the Navy's mile of chain-link and barbed wire; left again in front of B-Gate and onto 301, approaching Pope's Service Station from the North. The way the building was oriented I'd be able to see if there was a Cadillac in front of it.

There was no Cadillac. I drove a little way past the station and pulled over on the shoulder. There was nothing much out there, no businesses or houses or even much in the way of trees; it was mostly a patchwork of scrubby fields broken by the occasional line of oaks, ash and sweet gum, and fences covered in Virginia creeper, and you could see clear up to Cloverdale House.

The landscape was not conducive to sneaking around, but it was getting dusky and I thought I had a chance. I got my field glasses out of the glove box and walked back through the brush, which was waist-deep and offered some cover at least. I dislodged a couple of mourning doves, the air in their feathers making a trilling noise as they flew away. They were soon for bed anyway.

The bugs were getting louder now, their ode to a summer's evening reaching fever pitch. Ahead of me, behind a line of cedars, stood the green clapboard building with the gambrel roof. Beyond it I could see the back of the gas station, grey cement blocks, an electric meter, a couple of windows and an oil tank. A power line extended from the roof to a utility pole.

I jogged in a crouch and took cover in the gloaming between the trees and the clapboard hangar. I stopped to listen and didn't hear much besides the cicadas. There was a faint light from the left-hand window back of the service station. I didn't see any movement, so I crept around to the barn doors on the front of the hangar. They were padlocked and I felt too exposed on that side of the building.

I saw a glow coming down the highway and ducked back behind the line of cedars and watched a car drive by, headed south. It was not a Cadillac. I checked around and could find no loose boards or any other way into the barn. There was no Piper parked nearby, and no other aircraft that I could see. No lights were on inside the gas station.

The light wasn't great, but there was something going on out in the southwest end of the field, where the back runway terminated at the edge of the property. Unfortunately there were trees, brushy creek beds, and creeper-laden fences crosshatching the land between me and the far end of the upside-down L that was the airfield. It looked like part of a truck or maybe an older car, and there was movement, but I just couldn't tell what I was looking at.

I assumed they'd driven out across the runway, but I couldn't figure why. It was too late in the evening to be surveying anything. Then I remembered all the shoelace wrappers in the Hillcrest trashcans, and the mud-crusted toothbrush, and I wondered where Vasiliou and his boys had been tromping around, and what it might have done to their shoes. Vasiliou and the Hat seemed like the kind who'd have overshoes, but not so much Drakos. Which may have explained the toothbrush.

If they weren't surveying, what were they doing out there? It dawned on me just before I heard the aircraft approaching. I scrambled back to the truck, thankful for the dying light and the fedora pushed low on my head, and before I pulled away I saw a little yellow plane making what I thought was probably a risky landing in the tricky light of dusk. It would take a good pilot. One who knew the field. You probably couldn't move much cargo of consequence in a plane that size, but not all things of value were things of size. And not everything had to travel in bulk.

I pulled off the shoulder and out onto 301, then made an illegal U-turn without my headlights on, and stopped just before the creek. There on the west side of the highway was a grassy space with a couple of trees, and one headstone: James Lincoln Pope, Jr. June 1, 1896 – August 16, 1956. One day short of fifteen years after he'd bought the airfield. I had no idea what that meant, but it seemed significant.

I walked back to the truck and drove away. When I passed the gas station there was still no activity and no lights on, and I could see a hint of light out across the field, but I could make nothing out. I didn't linger. I was late meeting Ethel.

I took 206, mostly so I wouldn't have to drive past the Hillcrest in case the owner had called the Sheriff, because it had been long enough by now they'd have a car there if he had. I somewhat exceeded the speed limit and it took about ten minutes to get to Arnold's Corner and then I cruised on out Millbank Road and turned toward Gera. When I made my way up the dirt drive to the Burkitt place, my Hudson was nowhere in sight.

I eased through the turnaround in front of the house and back out the driveway, the silhouette of Franklin Burkitt in the rearview mirror, framed in his front door, wreathed in yellow light. When I got home, the Hudson was parked in front of my house and Ethel Burkitt was sitting on my porch.

"Harry Cogbill I was worried sick."

"How long have you been here?"

"Long enough."

"What'll your old man say?"

"Bunch of bad words, probably. I could come inside maybe for a cup of coffee."

"I don't think that's a good idea."

"Well for heavens sakes I wasn't planning to leave my overalls at the door."

"Jesus Ethel."

Ethel Marie Burkitt had wit like a backhoe: she could build you up, tear you down, or run you over, and it did not bother her particularly to do any of them. I could think of no one that I would rather spend time with at any hour of any day. This last part I told her, and she took my hand and led me into the house.

I made coffee and a late supper. I got a couple pots of water going, and while I waited for those to boil I sautéed onions and garlic in butter, using a saucepan, and then added fresh cream and diced tomatoes and let it simmer. I added penne pasta to one of my pots of boiling water. While I was doing this, Ethel played with the fox and asked me the thing I'd been avoiding for the last couple of days.

"What do you call the little guy?"

"He mostly goes by 'Goddammit.'"

She looked me in the eye and slowly shook her head.

"As in 'goddammit get out of there!'"

"Goddammit don't poop on the rug," she suggested.

"Goddammit get the hell off the drapes."

"Right. Well that will not do."

"We're open to suggestions."

"Why don't you name him after your Army buddy?"

"Rollie deserves better than to have a carpet-pooping fox named after him."

"Well don't hurt the baby's feelings, mister."

"It would not be appropriate."

"You haven't told me much about Rollie."

"He's dead. It's nobody's fault really. He was brave. He died bravely."

"Could he be related to Bob Taylor from the Owens market?"

"No."

"How can you be sure?"

"I'm sure, okay? I don't want to talk about Rollie, or the war, Ethel. I saw things I wouldn't sully your imagination describing to you. I did things I'm not proud of. I was not particularly brave or heroic, and the Germans? Most of them were just guys doing their duty to their country like I was. Killing some random Fritz wasn't the same as killing Hitler, Himmler, or Goering. There's nothing holy about it. The world is not a better place because Johann Schmidt died in a ditch with a Mauser clutched in his hands."

Ethel and the fox were both staring at me.

"You don't sound like a soldier."

"I never felt much like one either."

She put the fox down and got up and crossed the little kitchen and put her arms around me and just hugged me for a moment. Her head was pressed to my chest and I put my arm around her shoulders and kissed her hair.

"You're a good man, Hieronymus."

"I'm never sure."

"Stop it. You're a good man, and for God's sake stop doubting your worth."

With my free hand I plucked the fox off the counter where he was making a run at the food, and dropped him to the floor. Then that arm went around Ethel's waist and we looked at each other for a while. The pull was gravitational.

"We don't want supper to burn," she said.

"No, we don't."

We let go of each other, but a threshold had been crossed, and we both knew it.

She intercepted the fox on another attempt at the counter.

"Let's call him Fawkes."

"Fox?"

"Fawkes. Some of the Brits I knew told me about this weird holiday they have. Guy Fawkes Night. Guy was a soldier, and a dedicated Catholic, and I guess he got in with a group who decided to assassinate King James I because he was protestant."

"What happened?"

"Well, the government caught wind of it, and Fawkes was busted hiding a bunch of gunpowder that was intended to blow up parliament. So on the fifth of November they have bonfires and burn the fellow in effigy."

"And you want to name the baby after this man?"

"He's a plotter."

"He does get busted frequently."

"You have to admit it suits him."

Fawkes looked back and forth between us, listening to the whole exchange, smiling mischievously. I was glad he didn't know about gunpowder.

I mixed some dried minced onion and garlic in a bowl with paprika, oregano, thyme, and several different varieties of pepper, rolled a couple of chicken breasts around in it, and tossed them in the skillet with some melted butter. I added some grated parmesan and romano cheeses to my cream sauce, stirred them in, and with my second pot of boiling water, I steamed some broccoli.

I drained the pasta, made a bed of it on two plates, topped it with the alfredo sauce and the steamed broccoli, and then set my two blackened chicken breasts on a cutting board and sliced them diagonally, not quite all the way through into strips, and laid them, still clinging together, atop the two beds of pasta. I sprinkled some parsley flakes across the top in case Ethel wasn't already impressed.

"And here I thought you only knew how to fry things."

"I don't cook like this when it's just me. There's no fun in it."

"You don't think you deserve to live a little?"

"I like sharing experiences."

"If you say so."

There were several things I wanted to say, but I couldn't think of a way to do it without sounding trite. I thought she deserved better than flowery words and promises that would probably only sound like the importunities of a snake trying to get into her overalls.

"I like sharing experiences with you, Ethel."

She blessed the meal and we ate, and drank coffee and talked and when the fox stuck his head in the sink and licked the sauce out of the pan, we made faces at each other and laughed. One day I was going to take her on a real date, and not to a diner but out to Colonial Beach to a country music show and stroll along the boardwalk and hold hands like other people did.

When we said goodnight her waist was slender in my embrace, and I felt the swell of her hips and the softness of her lips when we kissed. Inside my chest felt like a steam locomotive and my loins were pulsing with electricity, and I knew she was waiting for me to say something or make a move, and I did not. So at last we let go of each other's hands and when she stepped down off the sagging porch she turned to face me and said, "come to church with us tomorrow Cogbill. Even God himself rested on the seventh day."

"Church? With you and your daddy?"

"And why not?"

"I don't think he likes me much, Ethel."

"Well that's astute. Reckon he knows what's on our minds. Come to church. I mean, forgive me, maybe you go to one of the other churches in the county. You said Fawkes was Catholic, are you Catholic?"

"No. Not at all."

"Come with us, please? For me."

"Okay. For you."

"Great! We'll pick you up at ten. We'll have a nice time, you'll see."

I was nearly asleep when someone jimmied the lock on the front door. The sound brought me back up out of the soup, but before I could arm myself, the fox screamed somewhere in the living room, a man's voice unleashed a stream of profanity I hadn't heard since the last time I saw combat – something involving the Lord's name and a sex act – and then a car peeled out of the driveway.

If you've never heard a fox scream, the sound is pointless to attempt to describe except to say that you'd believe any explanation ranging from the banshee to a satanic cult performing human sacrifice. Hearing it in the dark in a shabby old farmhouse in the dead of night would unman Superman himself. When I stumbled out of the bedroom, the front door was standing open and Fawkes was perched on the curtain rod looking pretty pleased with himself. He'd ruined the drapes but I didn't care. I guess this time it was Fawkes who foiled a plot.

CHAPTER SIX

IN THE MORNING I could find no particular clue about the break-in the night before. My assumption was that it was The Hat, but for all the evidence I had it could just as easily have been Drakos or J. Edgar Hoover or maybe Fidel Castro. My gut instinct wouldn't do me any good at the Sheriff's office. I hadn't slept much; even with a bookcase pushed up against the door I found it difficult to relax, and after the incident Fawkes had spent a good deal of time crashing around the house.

By sunrise I gave it up and made a pot of coffee, scrambled eggs and bacon, and toast, and gave Fawkes a bowl of dog food to keep him busy while I ate. Then I showered and put on a pair of tan wool slacks, a white shirt with a brown pinstripe, a brown herringbone vest, and a striped tie in gold and burgundy that matched my cordovan oxfords. I drank the rest of my coffee on the porch and just about ten o'clock I saw the Burkitt's truck coming up the dirt drive. I left my cup on the railing and stepped down off the porch to meet them.

Mr. Burkitt was driving, and he regarded me with the cold stare of a raptor as he stopped the truck and Ethel flung the door open and stepped out on the running board, in a checked dress with a white collar and little white gloves. She had a little hat tilted back on her head, and her hair was curled. She was all made up, lips and eyes and eyebrows too.

"Good mornin' Cogbill! I was afraid I'd have to bust down the door and wake you up."

I grimaced at her choice of words. We gave each other a sort of restrained hello kiss, and she got back in the truck, slid over into the middle, and let me in beside her. I pulled the door closed and without a word, Burkitt threw the truck into gear and whipped around the turnaround and back out the dusty road toward Gera. The radio was off and Burkitt just stared at the road with a face like a gargoyle, a sport coat and a necktie over a clean set of work clothes.

Ethel surreptitiously took my hand and squeezed it.

"Nice morning, isn't it?"

I said, "yep."

I could just about see the black mist around Burkitt; he wished he was anyplace else, or maybe that I was anyplace else. Maybe he was imagining launching me into the sun. At that particular moment, it didn't sound half bad to me.

We pulled up in front of Trinity, a Methodist church near the courthouse across from Morris Chevrolet. Next door was an Episcopal church called St. John's, all whitewashed brick, looking like it belonged in a New England whaling town. A parish house stood between them like a mediator. Trinity had a gravel lot and a big gnarly tree in front, near the cemetery gate. It was red brick, and it had a tin roof and a tall wooden cross rising from the pinched top of the louvred belfry.

The little yard was enclosed with a brick and iron fence, and an Aermotor windmill creaked lazily beyond the cemetery, the steel tower draped with creeper and trumpet vines, the broad tail gleaming in the morning sun. Burkitt parked nose-in along the fence, and turned off the engine. I opened the door and stepped down, then took Ethel's hand and helped her down. Burkitt turned and looked at me, and crooked a finger.

"Get in, Cogbill. Shut the door."

I did.

"I don't like you."

"I know."

"Ethel's young and maybe she's a little naïve, and I reckon that's my fault. Her momma died when Ethel wasn't but eleven. I've done the best I can. She's all I got. I'm not telling you this out of some sorry-ass need for sympathy. It's a warning."

"Yes sir."

"Cut the shit. You're not much younger than me."

"Right."

"I love my daughter. She's fond of you, God knows why."

"I'm not sure either."

"The only reason you're in this truck is because I respect her."

"The only reason I agreed to get in this truck is because I respect her too, Frank. I can only imagine what kind of man you think I am."

"The kind of man who's got no job and goes around seducing women half his age."

I opened my mouth and closed it again.

"If you hurt my daughter, in any way, I will hurt you worse. Are we clear on that?"

I sat there a moment, looking him in the eye. Part of me wanted to tell him how much Ethel meant to me, and the other part wanted to come across the cab of the pickup and squeeze his neck until his eyeballs shot out. I opened the door and crunched across the gravel, up the concrete step and in through the door, where Ethel was waiting in the vestibule. I shook hands with the ushers and accepted a bulletin, and she led me through another set of doors and into the sanctuary, where the space went clear up to the roof.

The carpet was burgundy, nearly purple, with a pattern like roses in a darker shade. Dark wood pews with white side panels filled the bright, airy hall, apart from a wide center aisle, and a pair of white lecterns stood on a raised platform at the head of the space, separated from the pews by a horseshoe altar rail, dark wood with flat, white-painted, rectangular beveled balusters on a raised, carpeted step for kneeling. Several gothic-style pendant lights hung on chains, and two matching wall sconces were affixed on either side of the sanctuary in the choir lofts. The whole thing smelled of a recent renovation. It was nice. There were five tall, narrow, bright stained-glass windows down each side. We sat about halfway down, on the left.

"Did he give you the talk?"

"We'll discuss it later."

Burkitt came in, finally, a bulletin clinched in his fist, and Ethel had wisely positioned herself to be between us again. The preacher's name was Epps. We sang three hymns and did a responsive reading based on Psalm 98. There were no sung refrains. The ushers took up a collection, we sang the Gloria Patri and the pastor made some remarks about trying to build a fellowship hall to host Sunday school classes, Sunday dinners, with indoor bathrooms and a nursery space for the children. It was still a ways off but the people had recognized the need and were committed to raising the money. I didn't see anybody that I really knew, although I recognized a few of the faces.

There was a judge, and the Elmers Morris, Senior and Junior, from the big store across the street.

We listened to a scripture reading and the Reverend Epps preached on Acts chapter 10, which was a story about a Roman officer named Cornelius and the Apostle Peter. It was about all those who honor God being equal in His sight. I could feel Frank Burkitt's discomfort as he shifted awkwardly in his place on the other side of Ethel. Ethel patted my hand and took hold of it and spared me a smiling glance.

After the service, Burkitt dashed out the door during the Threefold Amen and damn near ran over the ushers. Ethel introduced me around. The names and faces were all sort of a blur; there were farmers, local businessmen and scientists from the Naval Weapons Lab. There were the Morrises, of course, and a tall guy with a last name that sounded vaguely like some kind of Roman officer, and a whole mess of Clifts, tall, dark-haired guys with honest faces and proud Virginia accents, who shook my hand firmly and said "how-do."

We shook Epps' hand in the vestibule on the way out the door. I thanked him cheerfully for his message, and Ethel whacked me playfully on the shoulder. Burkitt had driven off. We got a ride from a fellow named Garrison who owned the garage out at Office Hall. I had an uneasy feeling the whole way down my dirt drive, and as we got close to the house I could see that my Hudson was gone.

"Stop the car."

Garrison braked smoothly and unhurriedly. I told Ethel to stay in the car, and Garrison to keep the car where it was, and then I jumped out and walked up the drive, crept onto the porch and walked around the house once, checking the doors and windows. Everything seemed intact. Even my tin cup was still on the railing. I went inside and found Fawkes sound asleep. I scratched his fuzzy cheeks and then went back outside, walked down the drive and got back in the car.

"They only took my car."

"Who'd steal a car way out here?" Garrison said.

"The same guy who broke into the house last night, probably."

"Lord, Cogbill. You need to go to the Sheriff."

"Believe I'd listen to Miss Ethel," Garrison said.

"It's a warning. Anyway I don't have a telephone."

Garrison looked back and forth at both of us, understanding that there was something he didn't know.

"What happened when they broke in, Harry Cogbill?" Ethel said.

"Nothing much. Fawkes like to scared the hell out of him, and he ran away."

"Am I in danger?"

"I hope not. I'm not sure. Probably not if you don't hang around here."

I didn't know if they'd been watching the house last night, or this morning, and if they'd seen Ethel or Frank. There was also the chance that the man from the Hillcrest had told Vasiliou and Drakos about the pickup truck, which would make things worse.

"I can bring you to my house let you use the phone," Garrison said.

"Let's take Ethel home first, make sure Frank is okay."

Ethel looked at me with a hint of panic in her eyes as Garrison put the car into gear and turned it around in front of my house.

"I got us into this."

I put my arm around her and held her.

"No you didn't. You're not responsible for what Vasiliou or Drakos or the man in the hat get up to. You're not responsible for your Uncle Jack's choices, or your grandfather's. You're also not responsible for mine, or Frank's. We all make our own choices here."

"Beg your pardon," Garrison said. "But what's going on?"

"There's a criminal element in this county," I said, "come down from up north. They're probably counting on the fact that there's not a lot of people around here and not a strong law enforcement presence."

"Always thought all the gangsters was out at the Beach."

"I think they're probably everywhere."

"We've had right much more burglary and such this last year," Garrison admitted. "Did you know someone broke in a couple rooms at the Hillcrest yesterday?"

"You don't say."

"Reckon that's why Sheriff Dishman retired. Worst he ever had to worry about was people driving too fast."

Garrison likely hadn't been among that number; it felt like he was doing all his driving in slow motion. Probably I was just anxious. The landscape in King George was definitely changing. Sam Dishman was not a young man, and he'd never seen any violent crime in the county.

When we pulled up at the Burkitt place, everything looked normal. The truck was parked in the turnaround and there were cows grazing in the far pasture. I could hear the chickens and the rattle of the Aermotor ginning.

"Maybe you'd better both stay here while I look around."

"No, let's both go," Garrison said. "Just in case. If you hear any commotion, Miss Ethel, you drive this car right out of here like the devil was on your heels, you hear me?"

"I hear you, Mr. Garrison, but I don't believe that'll be necessary."

We hadn't gone far towards the house when Frank Burkitt came out with a shotgun and pointed it at me.

"Garrison, take this son of a bitch off my property."

"Now Mr. Burkitt, calm down, for God's sakes it's Sunday. We come to check on you."

Ethel got out of the car and came to stand with us.

"I don't think I will calm down. Come over here, Ethel."

She didn't. We all stood there like that for what was probably a few seconds and felt like about a year. Frank reached in the hip pocket of his coat with his left hand and pulled out some folded papers pressed between two of his fingers. He kept the shotgun pointed at me with his right hand, the stock braced against his shoulder. He held the papers out toward Ethel.

"Take it. Go on."

"No daddy, I don't think I will."

"You don't know who this man is you've been running around with. I got this in the mail. Take it."

Ethel stood her ground.

"He's a coward, Ethel. He got two of his men killed in France. He let his best friend jump on a grenade for him because he was too scared to die. A man like that ain't worth your time. Now you come over here."

"Go ahead and shoot me, Frank."

"Daddy, no!"

"Just do it. That's what this is about, right? You're the bigger man, the hardass. Old iron nuts. Go ahead and shoot me if it'll make you feel better."

Ethel flung herself across me.

"Daddy Franklin don't you dare!"

He let go of the papers. The wind caught them and carried them from the porch into the lawn. He stood there for a while looking like the face of the demon that haunted my sleepless nights.

"Every one of you get out of here," he said. "Take Ethel with you. You win. She loves you."

She loved him, too. Murdering me would not have made him feel better. And she would have lost us both. I hoped he'd realize that when he calmed down. He turned and walked into the house, and eased the door shut. Ethel stood in front of me looking like she'd been slapped.

I'd never seen her so vulnerable. My proud woman with the iron backbone was crying softly, the sun was behind a cloud, and the wind in her hair was like the first portent of a coming storm. The papers Frank had dropped tumbled past my feet. I put a foot on them and bent to pick it up. It was a few sheets stapled together. Some highlights from my service record.

"I'm sorry you had to see that Mr. Garrison."

"Miss Ethel you don't owe anyone an apology. Come to my house, y'all can use the telephone and call the Sheriff."

"I couldn't possibly impose on you any further Mr. Garrison. I'll get the truck and take Harry Cogbill home. Maybe we'll have lunch. Would you care to join us?"

"I've got to be getting back to my family, but thanks all the same."

Ethel drove me back to my house and helped me fix lunch. She took off her hat and gloves; I remarked that I liked her outfit and she smiled, and suddenly the awkwardness and the frustration of the morning's violations had abated.

"What was that piece of paper my daddy had?"

"It was the reader's digest version of my Army career, mostly the low points."

"How does one get something like that? Seems like you'd need official channels."

"That's about the shape of it," I said. "Somebody's got connections. If Len ever gets back to me, maybe I'll know."

While we ate sandwiches and drank iced tea I asked her how long she thought it would take Frank to calm down.

"I don't know. I've never seen him like that. He ain't been right since Mama died and I don't think he's really got the handle of it, you know?"

"He thinks he's losing you too."

"Well for God's sake I'm a grown woman. I'll always be his daughter and he'll always be my daddy but he's got to learn to let go."

"Of both of you."

"Yep, that about says it."

When we were done eating and had not yet cleared the table, Fawkes dashed in and leaped up onto the counter and stared out the window, and we looked at each other and then outside and saw the Sheriff's car coming up the drive. I went to the door and heard Ethel rinsing off the plates. About the time the Sheriff stepped up onto the porch, Ethel came outside to join us.

The Sheriff was a short, stocky brick of a man with his dark hair slicked down under a brown octagonal hat. He wore a brown and khaki uniform and a gold star on his breast. His name was Powell.

He said, "Miss Burkitt, your father reported that truck as stolen."

"Well for Heaven's sake Sheriff, how can I steal my own truck? I drove Mr. Cogbill home on account of it's his car that's been stolen."

"Is that right, Cogbill?"

"Yes Sheriff, it was stolen out of my driveway while we were at church this morning."

"I see. You two go together?"

Ethel said, "that's right."

"You aware your truck matches the description of the suspected getaway vehicle for a recent burglary?"

"Sheriff do you really think my daddy or I would burgle anyone?"

"No ma'am, I cain't say as I do, but your friend Mr. Cogbill does fit the description of the man seen lurking behind the Hillcrest before he jumped in the truck and drove off. You wouldn't happen to know anything about that, would you, Cogbill?"

"Aw jeez, Sheriff, I think there's been a terrible misunderstanding. Miss Ethel had confided in me that she was concerned about some suspicious men hanging around her uncle's place, and being generally concerned for her safety and that of her family, I decided to take a look. I admit that I learned they were staying at the Hillcrest when I happened to stop there for lunch one day, and after they threatened me proper I decided to get a different car and come back, hoping to follow them on their daily activities and see if I could catch them doing anything worth bothering you about. Being a good citizen and all. Of course I'd had about a gallon of coffee and I'm afraid I had to take a leak.

"I didn't want to risk being noticed, or giving them time to get away, so I went behind the building to minimize the amount of time I spent away from my post. Even so, the manager almost caught me in the act and I was embarrassed, so I told him something about checking the meters and by the time I got back to the truck, the men had driven off and I didn't see which way they went. It was a rotten piece of luck."

"He said you had a prybar."

"I don't know what to tell you, Sheriff, he's plumb wrong on that account. I may have been carrying a newspaper, I don't quite remember. Wait, did you say there was a burglary? That old boy might have saved my life. Would you tell him I'm in his debt?"

The Sheriff's face was a mask. Neither of us was under any illusions about what I was full of, or how much.

"I got to go talk to Frank Burkitt about the legality of filing false police reports. In the meantime try not to take a leak behind any more businesses. And if you're thinking about leaving the county, take my advice: don't."

"He ain't going anywhere, Sheriff."

"Well Miss Ethel, if he's got any sense you're right. You look right pretty today."

"Thank you Sheriff. What I meant to say is he hasn't got a car, remember?"

"What was the make and model of your car, Mr. Cogbill?"

"It was a '53 Hudson Hornet. Two-tone robin's egg and white, but it was in pretty bad shape, I don't know why anyone would want it."

"What was the license number?"

I told him, and he wrote it down.

"Well, most times these things are sold for scrap and the thieves make some quick money. It's not likely you'll see it again, Mr. Cogbill, so I'd phone your insurance company as soon as you can."

"Thank you Sheriff. I think one of the guys staying at the Hillcrest did this. Somebody broke in my house late last night too. I think it was them."

Powell took off his hat and rubbed his face with his hand.

"What the hell is this county coming to?"

After the Sheriff left, Ethel and I sat on the porch a while.

"Would it be all right if I stay here tonight, Cogbill?"

"All right with who?"

"I've been thinking and I want to let my daddy sweat it a while. It might be the only way to get through to him, if he realizes how crazy he's acting."

"You don't have any things."

"I don't need things."

"I don't have a guest room. I can put on clean sheets for you, and I can sleep alright on the couch, but--"

"Harry Cogbill."

"But I'm not sure you're safe here."

"I am perfectly safe with you and you know it."

"These are evil men, Ethel. They know more about me than I do about them. They know we're together. They're using your daddy to get to me. I don't like how this is going. If anything happens to you..."

"You'll protect me."

"No matter what I do, everything always gets sideways and I can never turn it around."

"You know, other people have problems, Cogbill. We don't let it define us. You've got to learn to let go, too. For you it's past mistakes."

"Everything your father said about me, everything in those papers. It's true."

"And?"

"And nothing. Boot camp is designed to make soldiers. It's a factory that churns out grunts like bottles of Coca-Cola. It's supposed to be foolproof. But all their brainwashing never worked on me. I was a terrible soldier."

"You were too much you."

"It's my biggest flaw."

"Harry Cogbill it's your greatest asset."

Electricity filled the air between us. I looked into her eyes and she looked right back into mine, and an entire conversation took place without words. She stood up and took my hand, and led me into the house and to the bedroom. Her body was strong, but soft. Muscles bunched in her shoulders and rolled delicately under the soft velvet skin of her back as she unzipped her dress. Her hips were wide and her waist was taut, but she had slight pooch below her navel.

Then we were in each other's arms and outside of time, where seconds became hours and hours became minutes, and there was nothing else in the world but the two of us. Her scent was musky and I felt the sweat in her hair along the back of her neck when I placed my hand there. Afterwards I held her and she put her face an inch from mine and we looked into each other's eyes again, and I felt like a teenager, as though making love to Ethel had transported me to a time before all the burdens of adulthood and the pain of failure and of loss that had since stained my soul. I knew that I loved her, as surely as I knew that I did not deserve her.

Somehow the day slipped away with cups of coffee and long talks, and we showered and ate a late supper. It was late that night when Sheriff Powell knocked on my door. His car was parked in the driveway, the bubble light pulsing but his siren off. He reddened a little but politely avoided comment when he noticed Ethel wearing one of my shirts.

"Cogbill, get dressed and come with me. Evening Miss Ethel."

"Am I under arrest? I don't know what Frank told you, but..."

"Take it easy, Mr. Cogbill, this hadn't got nothing to do with Frank Burkitt. It's about your car."

"Come on in, Sheriff, while we get ourselves together."

"I'd prefer to stay here on the porch, if you don't mind. Miss Ethel don't need to come."

"I'd rather not leave her here in case the burglar returns."

Powell shook his head but said it was okay.

Ethel got back into her dress and I put on a clean shirt and a pair of khakis, and in a few minutes we got into the Sheriff's car and he drove us out to Office Hall. You could see the glow for a mile before we got there. The KGVFD was there, and the firemen from the NWL, and Colonial Beach too. What was left of Garrison's Garage looked like a portal to Hell.

Ethel said, "Oh my God."

"Garrison gave us a ride from church to Frank's place today."

"Come with me, Cogbill. Miss Ethel, you may remain in the vehicle."

I patted her hand, and she looked at me with her other hand clamped over her mouth. "You okay, Ethel?"

"Oh my God, Cogbill, what'd they do? What'd they do?"

I put my arms around her and held her for a moment, until she pushed away and assured me she was fine. Then I got out of the car and followed the Sheriff over to one of the fire trucks, which said KING GEORGE VOL. FIRE DEP'T. on the door and had a red bubble light whirling slowly atop the cab. The firemen were letting Garrison's place burn. It had died down considerably and the building was little more than a huge pile of smoldering rubble with what looked like a car in the middle of it. Could have been mine but it was difficult to tell. Powell led me over to where Garrison was standing with one of the firemen, a rangy guy with short dark hair and narrow features. I recognized him from church.

"Sheriff."

"Gene, this is Mr. Cogbill."

"Harvey, innit? Believe we met this morning."

"Harry. Believe we did."

He shook my hand firmly but did not say "how-do."

"Got a car in there Sheriff says might belong to you."

"We didn't leave any cars in the bay Saturday," Garrison said. "And that is for sure a Hudson Hornet."

"Gonna be a while before anybody can get in there and poke around," the Sheriff said. "But you lost a Hornet, and Gene here found one."

"That'll be my car," I said. "Do you believe me yet, Sheriff?"

"What I see is an unlicensed private investigator tracking dogshit all over my county. I'll grant you hacked off some bad guys, but you broke into their motel rooms, and you lied to me about it. Don't speak, we both know it's true. Even if I cain't prove it. I've a good mind to arrest you and take Ethel Burkitt home to her daddy."

"She's a grown woman, Sheriff. People probably ought to start treating her like one."

He took his hat off with his left hand, put his thumb and his finger of his right hand in his eyes and rubbed them.

"You're a real piece of work, Cogbill. Where the hell are you from, anyway?"

"Chesterfield, mostly."

"You wanted for anything down there?"

"No."

"Cain't hardly blame them. I don't want you either."

CHAPTER SEVEN

MONDAY MORNING we had a lot to do. I made us breakfast, corned beef hash and scrambled eggs, grits and toast, Ethel looking at me with wide eyes over the rim of her coffee cup, wearing only my shirt with the sleeves rolled up, her hair fluffing out unevenly from sleep. I had no words to tell her how beautiful she was, so I smiled at her and asked if her breakfast was okay.

"Well you sure weren't lying when you said it was your specialty."

It had taken us a while to calm down after the fire at Garrison's. Although Sheriff Powell had once again chosen not to arrest me, he'd repeated his instructions not to leave town.

"Don't worry, Sheriff. I intend to see this thing through to the end."

"I'm going to pretend I didn't hear that."

"There's something going on in this county. We're on the same side."

"That's where you've got it all turned around, Cogbill. I'm on the side of the law, I got a badge. I don't need you charging around like one of Robin Hood's Merry Men."

"Why are you determined to make me the enemy?"

"I think you need to ask yourself that question. Maybe Miss Ethel can explain it to you."

He drove us back to my house and left us in the yard. We laid in bed talking a while before Ethel finally drifted off to sleep, my arms around her, and after a while I followed her.

So after breakfast, we showered and dressed, and drove the truck out to the store in Gera where she picked up a few things to tidy her hair, and I picked up a paper. John noticed that Ethel was in her Sunday dress, but for once he kept his mouth shut. No word yet from Len, but it was early and I would check back later. While Ethel made herself presentable – her words, not mine – I dug through the classifieds in the Free Lance-Star and found what I was looking for. Then we went into town.

It was about twenty-five miles from my place to Fredericksburg. Route 3 was a long, two-lane country highway that wended its way through forests and farmland. We drove through the courthouse area and out past Arnold's Corner and Jeter's Lumberyard, through Comorn. To the north, Rokeby sat up on the hill overlooking the cornfields, a massive brick house with a hipped roof flanked by a line of trees like a rank of guards. Down by us on Route 3 an iron gate with stone posts marked the entrance to the driveway. A turnoff to our left was the beginning of Port Conway road, which looped lazily southwest, through Dogue and past Millbank, back toward 301 near the James Madison Bridge. Now Route 3 carved a tunnel through the forest, the trees overhead blotting out all but a twinkling of the bright morning sun, until we barreled out the other side at La Grange, the landscape opening back up to field and pasture.

Out by Graves' Corner at route 605 it was all farmland as far as you could see, big grey barns with tin roofs rusted red and purple. Near one of the barns sat a blue flatbed truck with pontoon fenders, loaded up with two rows of big tin milk cans. We were on a thin slice of land between the Rappahannock and Potomac Rivers, near the Stafford County line. Sometimes if you drove the road before dawn in late summer or early fall, the fog rolling off the water was so thick you couldn't see but a few feet in any direction.

We crossed the railroad tracks near Farley Vale, and entered Stafford still surrounded by farmland. Not long before Ferry Farm, where George Washington spent his childhood, the road rippled sharply up and down three times in rapid succession, a common feature of country roads of the type that my mother always referred to as thank-you-ma'ams. It always felt like a Carnival ride when you hit them at speed, your stomach lurching up into your diaphragm and slamming back down into your bowels, one-two-three.

We rounded a long, sweeping curve into Argyle Heights, a set of train tracks pulling parallel to the road, on a ridge above us to the right, then cutting away from the road and disappearing into the trees. To our left, across the Rappahannock, the tall brick stack of the FMC cellophane plant pumped its malodorous emissions into the blue sky. The stench, so oppressive it was nearly malevolent, carried on the wind and blew through Argyle Heights, the wet, putrid funk of wood pulp and sulfur like an outhouse on a sweltering summer day.

At Ferry Farm the road bent left toward the Rappahannock River, then peeled away right and snapped hard left again to dive through a narrow concrete arch below the train tracks and back up over the Chatham Bridge, above Scott's Island in the Rappahannock, and into downtown Fredericksburg beside the Old Stone Warehouse. We parked on the street near JC Penney, where Ethel picked up a few clothing items, and we strolled around town a while, enjoying the pear trees and mossy brick sidewalks, the green steeples of the churches rising high above the colonial architecture and warm shopfronts. Somewhere below the asphalt, the original cobblestones were still in the ground, like all of history an uneven foundation upon which the modern world is built.

Autumn was in the air, and a cool, gentle breeze rustled in the pear trees and the first of the leaves surfed the currents around us, clattering off the shop windows and swirling around entryways. We held hands and walked slowly, lingering at window displays and street corners, and for a morning at least, all the darkness of the world melted away and peace and comfort followed us like the rich, fruity scent of pipe tobacco along streets where Mary Ball Washington once walked, and James Monroe had practiced law, and the ghosts of Union and Confederate dead leaned on long rifles, smoking hand-rolled cigarettes in shaded doorways, pushing the brims of their kepis back to feel the cool air on their soot-darkened brows.

I used a payphone and called a guy from the want ads about a car he was selling somewhere in Spotsylvania, and set up a meeting for later that afternoon. Ethel picked up a few toiletries in Goolrick's Pharmacy, and we ate lunch perched on chromium barstools at the long Formica counter, while a thick-bodied woman in an apron and a hairnet fussed with a milkshake machine, and burgers and cheese sandwiches sizzled on a flat top grill.

A Packard eased on by outside, long and low, the sun gleaming off the whitewalls, the chrome hubcaps throwing patterns of light through the plate glass shop windows and haloing Ethel's hair as it passed, her blue eyes turning to me as she sipped cola through a straw, and I can remember no greater feeling of contentment, nor more perfect a moment, in the entirety of my life.

Outside of town we stopped at a sporting goods store that sold fishing rods and hunting rifles, parkas, fleece-lined caps and rubber boots. Ethel had selected a good quality shotgun, and by the way she cracked open the breech and inspected it, it was clear she'd been taught her way around a gun. Good job, Frank.

"Planning on shooting some deer?" the man asked.

Ethel looked meaningfully at me.

She said, "Call it home security."

"I'm not fond of guns."

"Well that's too damned bad, Cogbill. I won't have you chained to me while you're running around trying to sort this mess out. And I damn sure refuse either one of us to go on living in fear."

"Ethel, you're something else."

"Tell me something I don't know, mister."

The guy selling the car was out near Thornburg. He had it in a barn out behind an old farmhouse. It was a '51 Ford Crestliner in black and red, and he let it go pretty cheap. It was missing a hubcap and there were some cigarette burns on the front seat, but it was pretty solid and apart from a couple of minor dings and some missing insignia, it wasn't in bad shape.

I paid the guy, we shook hands, and I followed Ethel through some back roads to Route 17, and then east to Port Royal and up across the James Madison swing bridge into King George, past Emmanuel Church, looking like it belonged under somebody's Christmas tree. We took a left on Port Conway Road and then right on Millbank and back toward Gera. We left the truck at the house and she got into the car with me.

"Well," Ethel said as we pulled back out onto Gera Road, "this is a sight better than your old one."

It was late afternoon now, and we stopped by to see John again and got our mail.

"Your friend called a while ago."

"Tell me you took a message, John."

"Yes sir, I did, but all he told me was get you to call him back if it wasn't too late."

I looked at Ethel, and then at John. Must have been something big.

"Do you mind?"

"It's all right."

I dialed Len's office number but he was off-duty and the detective who answered the phone didn't have any idea what he might have for me and didn't much sound like he cared. I'd try back tomorrow. Ethel and I went home, fed Fawkes, and made supper together and sat on the porch while the sun bled out across the treetops, and the little brown bats performed a flying circus as they hunted insects in the dying light. It had been a perfect day, and all I wanted was to end it on a perfect note, to watch Ethel fall asleep as I held her in my arms and know that just for one single day, all was right in the world.

But of course, it wasn't. There was war ratcheting up in Vietnam, Castro in Cuba. Brave men and women in the south were being brutalized by police for standing up for their basic human rights. Ethel and Frank weren't speaking. And there were bad guys up to no good in Dahlgren, who had burned down an innocent man's business and destroyed a perfectly serviceable wreck of a car. I had one nagging question on my mind, and the only way I could think to answer it was under cover of darkness: what were they doing up at the back end of the airfield? What had been worth ruining shoes and laces over? What was Taylor's part in everything, out at the Owens Market? And how cross would Sheriff Powell be if he caught me trespassing?

I told Ethel what was on my mind.

"You want to go prowling around up behind my uncle's place?"

"I just got to decide how to get up there. Somewhere off Owens Drive?"

"Probably. But it won't be far back there. If you get to Hooes you've gone too far." She pronounced it "hose," not "whose."

"It's all farmland up there, isn't it?"

"Yeah, mostly. The airport is landlocked. They'd have had to make an arrangement with somebody, if there's a way to get a car in and out. Maybe Hud Avery."

"Hud?"

"Hud. Don't ask because I don't know."

I dug out my old combat boots, the leather worn dark and smooth, the laces swampy, the straps at the calf warped where they had always been buckled. I tucked the cuffs of my work pants into the tops of the boots, and put on my fedora and a mackinaw. I had an old gooseneck army flashlight, and I clipped it on my belt under the coat. Ethel had her shotgun and a box of shells, and she promised to make sure before she pulled the trigger that if somebody came in, it wasn't me.

She kissed me goodbye and I almost didn't go.

It was a long, lonely drive up to Owens. I took it easy, in case of deer, and it seemed like it took half an hour to get to the little intersection with the store and the Baptist church on cinderblocks. All the houses were dark, the Weedonville Post Office shut up tight, the moonlight blue on the tin roof of the frame house, a faint stream of wood smoke from one of the chimneys. A doe and two fawns in the field, eyes catching the light, watching as I drove past.

Skunk musk near Berthaville where maybe somebody had squashed one with their car. The odor followed me almost to Owens, and there at last was the little intersection, the church, the store. I turned left onto Owens Drive and followed the curve around to the north. I didn't have far to go before a dirt farm road went out in a straight line across the inside of the curve, toward the ridge line in the general direction of the airport. Cloverdale house sat out there, on the ridge, and there were farm roads running laterally along the ridgeline.

I left my car on the side of the road some distance away, killed the lights and the engine, and waited a few minutes. No traffic approached from either direction. Finally I got out, carefully climbed over the barbed wire fence, and crept across the fields in the direction where I reckoned the end of the back runway must be.

After what felt like another half an hour, I came to the ridge line, a safe distance from the darkened house with its low eaves and tall brick chimney, a gnarled sentry tree leaning out over the crest of the hill. Below me the land dropped away, a patchwork quilt of pasture and fences spreading down toward Pope's Field. Beyond that I could see the dark ribbon of highway 301, the lights of a single car heading north.

The moonlight shimmered on the Potomac river some four or five miles away, the red light atop the truss of the Morgantown bridge pulsed slowly, the beacon at Lower Cedar Point winking just beyond. To the east at the Naval Weapons Laboratory, there were red warning lights atop the checkerboard water towers. To my right a long, dirt drive ran down the hill, around a scrubby patch of saplings, toward 206 and Owens.

I took a deep breath. Once I stepped off the ridge I was hanging my ass out into space, far from help or safety should anything go wrong. But I was already beyond the point of no return, and there was absolutely no other way out from under Vasiliou and Drakos than to push on through. I felt the tension spread from my neck across my shoulders, my perfect day with Ethel like an episode from another man's life.

I put my head down, and descended into the shadowy fields, picking my way down the hillside among the cowpies. I skirted a small oblong agro pond, and picked up an access road, slicing off to the left. The field was long, but the weariness I felt had nothing to do with the hike. And there in the cold blue moonlight I saw him, a wiry man in army fatigues, humping his pack and an M1 Garand cradled in his arms, his BDU's pursed into canvas gaters. His head turned, his dark face nearly invisible in the long shadow below his steel pot, just two dimly twinkling points of his eyes and the cherry of a cigarette. He may have smiled, never breaking stride; then he turned his gaze away. I thought sometimes he had come to lead me across the veil into the next world; other times I did not believe he was real.

It must have been another twenty or thirty minutes, following the dirt road across the field like a swimmer out at sea, a couple of old trees looming ahead of me, the soldier to my right, until like smoke he just dissolved into the shadows and was gone. And there at last it was, a back way into Pope's Field, not part of the access road but a neatly mown swath wide enough for a car, that looped around one of the trees and then made a turn at the other, and from there ahead of me was wide open land, the filling station a light blur in the moonlight, out across the blue-green pancake.

There were dried footprints in the earth, and parallel tracks of tires where the grass was flattened down and silver in the moonlight. I wondered why you'd need a back way in and out of the airport, especially one that cut across a farm and accessed out onto a back road. I wondered what they could possibly be moving in small aircraft. Marijuana? My aunt Ida's stamp collection? Maybe when I talked to Len, he'd have some useful information for me.

When I got home, Ethel watched discreetly from the door, saw by the glow of the porch light that it was the Crestliner, and then met me at the porch.

"You didn't have to wait up, Ethel."

"No, but I wanted to. Besides, who can sleep with Fawkes crashing around? Find anything?"

I told her about the easement from the back runway to the Avery place.

"Why would they need that? Assuming they're shipping goods, don't they usually have a good cover story? And how much freight can you move in a small aircraft?"

"See, those were my questions too." And whatever it was, they were pretty serious about it.

I locked the front door and checked all the other doors and windows, turned off the lights as I went. Then we undressed and I held Ethel close, her back to my chest, her hands clutching my arm to the softness of her breast, and I listened to her breathing, felt her body rise and fall, and clung to her as to life itself.

The following day, after breakfast, I went out to the store in Gera and borrowed John's phone. This time I got Len at his desk.

"Hey, don't ask me for no more favors, all right? Forget my number. You wouldn't believe the IOU's I had to cash in for this crap. I wish you'd called a contact with the fibbies."

"I don't know any Feds, Len."

"Yeah, well, suddenly I do. I asked around about Nikolaos Drakos and the FBI climbed right up my ass. What'd you get me into, Cogbill?"

"I wish I knew. Tell me you got something for me."

"None of these guys has a sheet in Boston, but I made some calls. Baltimore tells me Vasiliou was in the Marine Corps in World War II, maybe you got a contact can run that down. He don't live there no more, change of address to someplace called Anne Arundel County. Adagio's an attorney from Brooklyn, New York. Looks clean. Can't find anyone called L. Thomas Boone at all.

"Your friend with the hat is probably Nestor Lazos. They know him in Baltimore, he's got a record in Philadelphia going back to childhood. Mostly petty theft and assault. He's a known associate of your Mr. Drakos. Both of them have records thicker than the damn Boston telephone directory. Watch out for Lazos. He's a suspect in about eight unsolved murders between Baltimore, DC, and Philadelphia."

"He didn't seem that smart."

"Smart? No. Connected. Both of them. Drakos has been in trouble for fraud ten times in the last twenty years. His lawyer got him out of four of them in trial, they were able to appeal the other six. Way this guy skates he should be in the Olympics."

"Let me guess, he's a 'legitimate businessman.'"

"Yeah, I think that's the technical term."

"Greek mafia."

"They mostly run drugs. You got a lot of addicts out there in the sticks?"

"Who would notice?"

"Two squirrels and a possum."

"Right. Hey Len?"

The line was dead. He'd hung up on me.

When I got home, Ethel was in my bathroom in her bra, doing her makeup.

"What's the occasion," I said.

"Do I need an occasion?"

"No. I guess I'm used to overalls and plaid shirts."

"I knew it, you think the overalls are sexy."

"Ethel, you're beautiful in anything."

"Well since I ain't feeding chickens and forking poo today, I thought I'd dress up a little."

I asked her if she wanted to ride up to Waldorf with me, and to my delight she said yes. So I had coffee and read the paper while she finished getting ready, until she joined me in the kitchen in heels with a new pair of capri pants and a sweater, her hair clean and curled and smelling of strawberries. I gassed up the Crestliner at the Morris's store and we went out to Office Hall, where Garrison's Garage was a heap of burned timbers and grey ash, staked off by the Sheriff's office and the State Police, and turned north onto 301 past the Stuckey's Pecan Shoppe. She asked me what I'd learned from Len, so I filled her in as I drove, Vasiliou the former supply sergeant and a complete mystery; Drakos and Lazos, the hoods with extensive criminal histories.

"And what's in Waldorf, other than a bunch of liquor stores, casinos, strip clubs, and seedy motels?"

"No, that about covers it. But I used to work in one of those casinos, and my old boss might talk to me."

"You think they're running drugs out of my family's airport?"

"I don't want to make any wild accusations."

"Well for heaven's sake, you're not going to offend me."

"I don't have any evidence."

"But?"

"Drugs would be one of the few things that could be moved in relatively smaller quantities and still command a large return of investment."

We were traveling north on 301. We went around the traffic circle at Edgehill and through Allnut and up the hill at Owens, past the Hillcrest and down the hill again toward Dahlgren, the filling station, the little airport and the Pope family cemetery and over Williams Creek. Gate B for the NWL was on the right, and soon Wilkerson's Potomac Grill on the left, where we'd had our first date, across the street from a tall chain-link fence with a few strands of barbed wire angled out at the top and signs marking it as Federal land.

Ahead on the right, beyond the fence, a tall building looking like a weirdly sinister mill or grain silo alone on a hill with the words US NAVY on it, overlooking the river; to the left, Wayside Park, and then the sound of the road under the wheels pitched up as we mounted the Morgantown Bridge.

Our windows were rolled partway down, and Ethel watched the ground drop away from us, her hair fluttering in the air that was whipping around our ears. She turned to face me and I could feel her electric blue gaze although my eyes were on the narrow stretch of bridge rising slowly ahead of us.

"Did Nestor Lazos kill my granddaddy?"

"I think somebody did."

"I think it was Lazos."

"I think you're probably right," I said.

The railings on either side of the bridge were tubular steel and painted battleship grey, and at speed our view of the river was mostly unobstructed. The river below was blue, the channel for larger ships leaving Alexandria staked out clearly with signs about a mile out. Floats from crab pots bobbed in the shallows, and out to the right the Lower Cedar Point beacon flashed at intervals, a skeleton tower with a green marker on the foundation of an old screwpile lighthouse that had been dismantled only a few years before.

The bridge went out for a mile or so with a slow, steady incline and then the huge steel beams of the truss rose on either side of us, the color of an aircraft carrier, lined with huge rivets, criss-crossing above us and all around, the red beacon on the highest point far above our heads, on a catwalk only accessible by an enclosed ladder that spidered up the side of the truss. We were above the channel now, at the zenith of the bridge's arc, where barges and ocean liners could pass beneath us. There were none of these today, but away to the west the river was dotted with sailboats and small fishing boats, some rigged with outboard motors.

And then the bridge angled down, a much steeper approach on this side, with maybe half a mile's distance to get back down to ground level, a marina on the left and on the right, trees and uninterrupted coast line, with a few small cottages visible out near Morgantown and in the grey distance at Swan Point. The sound of the wheels changed again, and a sign welcomed us to Maryland, and then Maryland took some of our money at a toll booth for the privilege of crossing their bridge, and we charged on into Charles County.

Up here route 301 was a four-lane divided highway, new enough that if it were a car it would probably still have the smell. We rounded the bend at Newburg, and through farmland at Allens Fresh and Faulkner, a Horne's Restaurant and Gift Shoppe all alone on the right with the sun blasting off its yellow roof, then a small motel and the school in Bel Alton, a long, pale building, low and flat-roofed, sitting in a hollow down from the road, a tall chimney rising behind it.

It was open country until we hit the town of La Plata, the county seat, but the new 301 bypassed the town apart from a Howard Johnson's on the southwest corner of the Route 6 intersection, and the odd filling station along the way. Then there was nothing again until we crossed the train tracks at White Plains and rolled into Waldorf: not as glamorous as Vegas, a strip of highway where hopes and dreams went to die. Owing to the local laws about alcohol, there were liquor stores seemingly on every corner. At night all the motels, with names like Stardust and Cadillac, would light up in bright neon and the clubs that lined the road would come to life with signs advertising live music or topless girls. In the daylight it looked like a parking lot full of UFO's.

We pulled up outside the Wigwam Casino, next door to the Stardust Motel. It wasn't a wigwam; it was a big building with a conical glass structure front and center built to resemble a giant tipi. There was a painted metal chimney at the peak that would puff out smoke for added effect. I doubted the natives would approve. Probably nobody had consulted with the local Piscataway tribe.

"You used to work here?"

"Yep. Mopping floors, mostly."

"Why did you quit?"

"You mean why did I get fired."

"Now Cogbill, you forget who you're talking to? The man may have fired you, but I know damn good and well you dared him to do it."

"Probably."

She winked and patted my thigh.

I went around her side of the car and took her hand and closed the door for her and she looped her arm through mine and we stepped up onto the pebbled sidewalk and around the corner to the door. It was still early and they were setting up for the night's entertainment. There were roadies setting up monitors, amplifiers and mic stands on the bandstand. A middle-aged guy in a t-shirt and khakis, with a cigarette in his mouth and his dark hair slicked down, came rushing over.

"Hey! Hey, we're closed here, huh? Get outta...Harry?"

"What's up, Bobby?"

"Harry Cogbill, no shit – pardon me, miss. How do you do? Name's Robert Campbell, but everybody calls me Bobby."

Ethel just stared at his offered hand until he retracted it.

"Ethel Burkitt," she said. Her tone of voice could have frosted hot coffee.

"Bob, is Stevie around?"

"Yeah, he's in the office, but be sure and knock and don't just bust in like you did in here, okay?"

I led Ethel around to the left and through a back section with a couple of smaller rooms to a door marked "PRIVATE." I knocked a couple of times and heard Stevie holler to come in.

I opened the door and saw that Stevie was alone, and then let Ethel precede me into the room. Little Stevie Balaban was the manager, and he sat behind a desk covered in paperwork, doing the previous night's receipts on a calculator with a spool of paper spilling onto the floor.

His jacket and tie were on a coat rack, his shirt was unbuttoned and he had a strap undershirt underneath, and a thin gold chain around his neck. A pile of cigarettes smoldered in a copper ashtray the size of a dinner plate. He needed a shave and by the look of his eyes a few hours' sleep wouldn't kill him either.

"Cogbill? Christ, this better not be about a job."

"Ethel Burkitt," I said, "Stavros Balaban."

"Stevie," he said. "You can sit down if you want. Not you, Cogbill."

Ethel and I both sat down anyway.

"It's not about a job," I said.

"Great. She's a mathematician and you heard about the little fiasco we had last night."

"I'm not a mathematician," she said. "Although I was an A student."

"Great," Stevie said. "Maybe you can teach this one some common sense."

"Maybe we should come back later," I said.

"Nah," Stevie said. "You know what? Here." He picked up the metal trashcan beside the desk, and with an arm, swept the papers and the calculator and a couple of pens and a bottle of correction fluid into the bin. "There. All my problems are gone. Screw it. What do you want?"

"Mister Balaban," Ethel said, "I hope we're not inconveniencing you. I can see you're having a rough morning, and I understand you have responsibilities here."

"Miss Burkitt, believe me, I could use a break from last night's disaster and as long as Cogbill here is serious about not looking for a job, I'm all ears for the next ten or fifteen minutes."

"Thank you, Mister Balaban."

"Seriously, call me Stevie. And if Cogbill here has sense enough to propose to you, bear in mind that you're better than he is."

"Well, thank you Stevie."

"I remind her every day," I said.

"I'm sure you do. So what's up, Harry?"

"I guess I'm looking into a family matter for Ethel here, and some names came up that I thought maybe you could give me some background on."

"That depends on what kind of names, and you know it."

"Dimitrios Vasiliou."

"Ah shit, Cogbill."

CHAPTER EIGHT

LITTLE STEVIE searched his desk, and the pockets of the rumpled suit coat on the coat rack, and finally stepped out to buy a fresh pack of cigarettes from the vending machine in the hall. When he came back he lit up from a book of matches stamped with the Wigwam's nomenclature, and threw the match in the ash tray.

"How in God's name did you get mixed up with Jimmie Vasiliou?"

"I'm not mixed up with him."

"Then you run afoul of him, which is almost as bad. You sure you want Miss Burkitt in here for this?"

"I'm a grown woman, Stevie."

"Yeah, and Jimmie Vasiliou is a grown crocodile."

I said, "So you know him?"

"We grew up together in the District."

"You're friends?"

"No, we're not friends, we grew up together. Same street, same hangouts, like that. Run with the same guys."

"He mobbed up?"

"He's connected. He's not a made man. He's what you call a fixer."

Ethel said, "A fixer?"

"Yeah, he helps people get what they want. Sets up transactions. For a price, you know."

"That doesn't sound so bad."

"You don't know Jimmie. You're doing dealing with Jimmie, only person who's happy is Jimmie. When we was maybe ten, I had this bicycle. Saved up for it, old man helped me buy it. Guy at the shop put it on layaway so I could pay for it a piece at a time, right. Took me a year. Jimmie wanted that damn bicycle.

"He could always find a way to make a nickel shelling peas or sorting produce. He'd work as a delivery boy. But when we was ten he got himself a paper route, and that bike was looking pretty good to him. I'd worked my butt off for that bike, and I wouldn't sell it to him.

"Well, my mom had bought me a radio for Christmas when I was eight. Nothing fancy, basically a box little bigger than a lunch pail, handle on the top, picture of the Lone Ranger on the dial. Little Bakelite job. We used to listen to ballgames in the summer and radio shows, you know.

"Well after I wouldn't sell the bicycle, he got a buddy of his over and wouldn't you know the idiot drops my radio out the window. Second floor, busts in a million pieces all over the sidewalk. Says it's an accident. I'm beside myself, right. Then Jimmie comes up with this deal.

"He'll get me a new radio. Better than the old radio. All I gotta do is give him my bicycle. He makes good on the radio. Didn't last me a month, the wires inside were all corroded. But he got that bicycle. And wouldn't you know I found out later he convinced his cousin to give him that radio. And my little Pilot, with the Lone Ranger on it? He had his buddy break it. I know he did. He wanted that bike. He got it, too."

"You still fr...uh, do you know him to talk to now?"

"Know him? Sonofabitch paved the parking lot."

"You hired him?"

"I didn't have a choice, he made a deal with my boss."

"Got it. I heard he served in the Corps during the war."

"You hear a lot of stories about Jimmie. Half of them might be true. He claims FDR invited him onto his yacht at the Navy Yard for breakfast one morning when he delivered him a paper."

"You believe it?"

"I believe he knows where the Navy Yard is. I believe he used to deliver newspapers."

"Right."

"I believe he eats breakfast."

"I get the picture."

"I believe he saw a picture of FDR once."

"You don't think he was a Marine?"

"Sure, poor kid from the block? Everybody served."

"Supply sergeant, is what I heard."

"Yeah, yeah I could see that. Look, I don't know anything about his service. I'd bet he ran a side hustle though."

"Right. He'd have access to all sorts of stuff. Uniforms, gear. Weapons. The military is worse at tracking that stuff than you'd think."

"Bet he brought some things in, too."

"Like what?"

"Cogbill, you were in the army, right?"

"Sure."

"Any of the guys in Europe ever smoke a joint?"

"Yeah, of course."

He made a face.

"Yeah, I get it. Stevie, reefer's cheap to produce, moves cheap too. It's easy money but it's probably not a path to riches or anything."

"You're not thinking like Jimmie, Cogbill. You know what's better than money? It's when the guys trust you because you get them what they want. And then—"

"And then you can groom them for...what?"

"Maybe he dealt in a little more than old combat boots and trench tools."

"Don't tell me any Nazi gold stories, Stevie. Guy had Nazi gold he wouldn't be paving roads."

"Sure he would. Hot-mix asphalt? Lots of creative uses for the kind of friends Jimmie's got."

I thought of Nestor Lazos and shivered. Ethel had a grip on my knee so tight I might never walk again.

"Ever heard of a guy named Nestor Lazos?"

Stevie looked at me for a long moment, then picked up his trash can and dumped it out on his desk.

"Now if this damn calculator still works maybe I can figure out what the hell happened here last night."

"Stevie."

"Math was never my thing, you know how it goes. You hire guys to handle it, they get lazy, you get burned. If anyone ever tries to make you a manager of anything, Cogbill, tell them where they can stick it."

I was looking hard at Stevie but he wouldn't meet my eyes.

"Come on, Stevie."

Without looking up he said, "if you've got Lazos coming at you I can't do nothing. Get on a plane to Honolulu. Or better yet Mars. I heard his mother gave him a puppy for his birthday when he was six."

"So?"

"Trust me. You don't want to know."

Ethel's hand was still on my knee and the other one was on my arm and although she did not do any permanent damage, for a while I wasn't sure. She was a strong girl.

"Now if you'll excuse me, Hieronymus, I've got a lot of work to do here."

"Have you considered burning the place down and absconding with the insurance money?"

"Way ahead of you."

As Ethel and I slipped out the back door to the side lot where we'd left the Ford, she said, "he won't really do that, will he?"

"Stevie? Not a chance. Probably."

Ethel was quiet as we drove out of Waldorf. Finally, somewhere around White Plains, she said, "Are you sorry you decided to come find me that day?"

"Why would I be?"

"Well, everything I got you into. The mob and maybe smugglers and who knows what."

"Ethel my life is better with you in it. Everything else is incidental."

"Are you sure?"

"Ethel Marie why wouldn't I be sure?"

She looked distracted, staring out the glass at the landscape of southern Maryland. Somehow I doubted she was really seeing any of it.

"You used to work for that man?"

"Balaban? Yeah. For a few months anyway. Didn't last long."

"You didn't know that he knew Vasiliou before we walked in there?"

"No, not really. Call it more of an instinct."

Ethel was quiet again.

"Is Stevie in the mob?"

"Hell, I don't know. Maybe. He knows guys. You know how it is. Business like that, a casino, night club...attracts a certain kind of attention."

She picked at some lint on her sweater, and watched the trees go by.

"You've made some weird choices in your life, Harry Cogbill."

"Yeah. Reckon I have. What's with the third degree, Ethel?"

"Did you ever think you're determined to punish yourself for something you did?"

"What kind of man do you think I am?"

"I know what kind of man you are, Harry Cogbill, or I wouldn't have gone to bed with you. The question is what kind of man do you think you are?"

I didn't say anything for a while as La Plata slipped by around us.

"I just don't want to be part of your penance," she said.

I put my arm around her shoulders and pulled her close. Ethel patted my thigh and leaned against me and although I could feel her warmth and smell the strawberries in her hair I had never felt more alone.

* * *

That night I took her to Colonial Beach to see Patsy Cline perform at Reno Pier. I thought a date night might do us both some good, or so I told myself. In reality I suspect I was trying to forget about the way Ethel had ripped open my fuse-box and pulled out a bunch of wiring. It was one of her particular talents and I do not deny that I loved her for it, although at times a kick in the pants would have been more comfortable.

There was also the matter of money; I was running low on it and since Ethel was no longer living with her father, at least for the time being, she was also cut off from her allowance. When I brought this up, rather delicately I thought, Ethel only said "the Lord will provide, Cogbill," and that was the end of it. I chose not to list our sins, but I don't believe either of us were oblivious to them.

So we drove out to the Beach, which was more or less due East, in Westmoreland County. We took 205 to Edgehill, went around the traffic circle and resumed 205 heading east, past Baker House on the right and Carruther's Corner, Alden and Ninde, and Tetotum Road, until we crossed Goldman Creek and the view opened up to the left, looking out across the Potomac, the Morgantown Bridge visible on the horizon beyond a little restaurant called Wilkerson's with a boat dock in back and a gravel lot just off the road. The road continued East for a few miles, and then forked at an area known as Beach Gate, either staying on 205 and looping to the right around a large Texaco station with a hipped tin roof, and off to Monroe Hall and Oak Grove beyond, or, as we did now, making a hard left onto Colonial Avenue, and into the little town.

We went straight back a few blocks, past some other filling stations, rental bungalows and a barber shop, the Potomac River black and shiny directly ahead of us beyond the boardwalk, under the light of the moon. On the left were a Masonic Lodge and Westmoreland Sundries, the latter a two-story clapboard building with a corner door and a double gallery. We turned right just before Westmoreland Sundries, onto Washington Ave. There was an Amoco on the left corner, a railroad-style diner on the right.

On a rise behind the Amoco to our left was the very large, pale yellow structure of the Colonial Beach Hotel. The middle portion of the Hotel was an old mansion that had once been the summer estate of Light Horse Harry Lee, who had been the master of Stratford Hall further down the river. There was a pool and an amusement park beside the hotel, with a scaled-down train called the "Little Reno Special" that ran all around the park and through a tunnel by the pool. We turned left off Washington Ave and headed straight back, toward the huge parking lot for Reno, a 24-hour club and casino perched on stilts out above the river.

It was sometime around 1949 when Delbert Conner brought gambling to the Beach. Gambling was legal in Maryland and the Maryland state line was on the Virginia side of the Potomac, so he built his business out over the river and loaded it down with slots, and a Roulette table. The pier, dubbed Reno, was the size of a football field. In less than a decade he had transformed Colonial Beach from a sleepy old steamboat destination, and the quiet summer home of Alexander Graham Bell, into a shimmering, thriving vacation destination – and transformed himself from the cash-poor owner of the Ambassador Hotel to a multi-millionaire whose establishment regularly hosted celebrity musicians. He'd had two grand pianos installed just for Guy Lombardo and the Royal Canadians.

Conner flew his guests in from DC on his Champaign Cruiser, a pink Boeing 247, to Reno Skypark out on 205 near Monroe Hall, and then ferried them from the little country airport up the road to the Beach in his pink Limousine. Visitors came to the Beach by boat, where many businesses had private docks and where it was possible to stroll up and down the boardwalk, shaded by willow trees, and enjoy sno cones and soft drinks and swim on public beaches encircled by jellyfish nets.

But in 1958, the State of Virginia had had enough. Colonial Beach was regarded as a den of sin, and the technically-legal workaround to allow gambling on Virginia's shores had become an intolerable blight in the eyes of preachers and politicians across the Old Dominion. The governor of our fair state, Mr. Thomas A. Stanley, caved to political pressure and applied a little pressure of his own to Maryland Governor Theodore McKeldin, and the state of Maryland banned gambling on the piers.

So this early autumn evening in 1959, as the Beach was winding down for the season, we found the little resort town in the early stages of a major identity crisis. We parked in the huge lot near the Reno Amusement Park, all light and sound, roller coasters, Ferris wheel, and merry-go-round, and watched the "Little Reno Special" go chugging by, the driver in his shirtsleeves with his black hair slicked down, his upper body sticking out of the top of a locomotive the size of a bobsled.

We crossed the lot and the concrete pad of the boardwalk, and up the gently sloping planks to the white façade of Little Reno, the name emblazoned in red above the entrance. Inside there was drinking and dancing, but no longer any gambling. I paid the cover charge and winced as more of my money went away.

We ordered drinks at the horseshoe bar on the left. There were empty platforms off to the right, sort of the middle of the room, where the slots used to be, and pinball machines across the front of the room under the plate glass windows. If you could sense, back in King George, that change was coming, out here in Colonial Beach you didn't need to sense it at all. It was all around you, and although the gambling had only been gone since the previous year, the signs were starting to show all across the colorful little town that hard times were ahead.

There was a sudden burst of hearty laughter and I saw Conner himself sitting down the bar, a large man in a finely-tailored suit, with dark hair and a healthy red color in his face, sharing a laugh with a few other local businessmen. Maybe they thought they could hang on. Maybe they knew they couldn't, and there was nothing left to do but laugh.

Ethel and I took our drinks and headed to the big room in the back, to the music hall and the stage where stars like Guy Lombardo and Jimmy Dean had been known to perform. I sensed this was the last time Patsy would be here as well. Without gambling, revenue was down and was likely to keep going down, and Cline's star was on the rise.

Her career didn't span more than half a dozen years, and in '59 she hadn't yet reached the heights of fame that she would soon achieve. I believe she and her husband Charlie Dick had just moved their family to Nashville, and soon she was to leave Four Star and be signed by Decca Records, but all of that was in the future, and though she'd appeared on the Opry and had been touring since arriving on the scene in '57 she had still only ever had one hit. That was "Walkin' After Midnight."

Patsy took the stage in a befringed cowgirl outfit, all boots and tassels and a wide-brimmed hat on a drawstring, red scarf knotted at her throat. There were a mix of styles, and not all of them really showcased her vocal talent, which may have been the reason none of them had charted. She did "I've Loved and Lost Again," and "Come On In," and the rockabilly number "Gotta Lot of Rhythm in My Soul." She sang the hell out of all of them, and when I looked at Ethel she was smiling and nodding her head and she took my hands and we danced to a few songs, feeling free and clear and far from all the drama of the last few days.

Patsy thanked us all for coming out and thanked Mr. Conner for hosting her and her band, and introduced the next number as a pop song a few of us probably knew, and then the piano tinkled out the opening notes of "Walkin' After Midnight" and regardless of her feelings about the song, she belted it out with the authority of an angel of the Lord. She had thick, dark hair and strong features, and a mouth that sort of pouted even when she smiled. When she sang she arched her left eyebrow a little and her eyes smoldered the way her voice did on her most powerful vocals, and after a particular line here and there she'd nod succinctly as if to let you know she thought she'd nailed it. I don't believe anyone would have disagreed.

Ethel and I held on to each other and in a jangly mix of piano and steel guitars, and the heights and power of Patsy's voice, it seemed our troubles had gone away. This was only a pretense, though, and the illusion was soon to break, and I would feel foolish to have believed that we could take a night to ourselves and not expect the harsh realities of the world we had stumbled into to visit their evil upon us.

It happened during "Three Cigarettes in an Ashtray." A voice in my ear said, "this do beat a barn dance, don't it?"

The speaker's mouth was against my ear, and I could feel the warmth of his breath in my ear canal. It was like a forced intimacy, a kind of violation of my person, and when I turned my head I found myself looking directly into the face of Nestor Lazos.

For the first time, I noticed that the proportions of his face were all wrong. His eyes were too close together and his jaw was too long, his lips a couple of sausages fattening in a skillet. His ears were jug handles below the porkpie hat. The eyes were green and hooded, set way back in his skull, and although his mouth was grinning his eyes were flat and cold, reptilian, as though they carried an ancestral memory of violence and death as arcane and elemental as the primordial ooze from which he'd crawled.

"What's shaking, Nestor?"

"Hey, you learned my name. All right. Bet you think that makes us even."

"Not intellectually," I said. There was a voice in my head telling me not to torque him, but I couldn't quite hear it over all the klaxons. I believe the klaxons were also in my head. I'm not sure what that says about me. "You could have brought five more and you wouldn't be equal to a plate of steamed crabs. They're also bottom-feeders. That means they eat ocean garbage. I'll let you work that one out."

My voice sounded distant and tinny, as though it belonged to someone else and had been broadcast through a short-wave radio in the back of my skull.

"I didn't see your car outside, Mr. Cogbill. You get a new heap?"

His grin widened to a toothsome smile, too broad for his face.

"What do you want, Nestor?"

"Mister Vasiliou has a proposition for you."

"I'm not interested."

"Well you haven't heard it yet."

"I'm not interested."

Ethel tugging on my arm.

"Cogbill let's go."

"Your girlfriend will want to hear this too."

"I don't believe I care to."

"You heard her, Nestor. Take off."

"I'm sure she wouldn't want anything to happen to her uncle."

That did it. Ethel still had my arm in a death grip, but she leaned across in front of me to look Nestor in the eye.

"What did you say?"

"See, Mr. Cogbill? I told you she was interested. You just got to know what a lady wants to hear."

"Come out with it, Nestor."

"We been very gentle so far in how we dealt wit' you, that's on account of Jack Pope. Your lady's uncle. He insists he won't work for Mr. Vasiliou if anything happens to his niece. Mr. Vasiliou and Mr. Drakos has what you call a counter offer. You back off their jocks and nothing happens to Jack. Nice and easy, right? You two can go on screwing and asking God to forgive you on Sunday morning, nobody cares. Well, 'cept Frank I guess."

"You take my daddy's name out of your mouth!"

"Come to think of it, I don't believe Jack indicated he gave a shit about Frank one way or the other. Anyway, consider the offer. Enjoy the show."

He winked at Ethel and stalked back into the crowd.

I looked at Ethel and tried to speak. I wet my lips and she stared at me with wide blue eyes, still clutching my arm.

"I guess we should go," I said.

"And let that creep ruin our night? He was vulgar and rude and will be until the day they put him in the ground. Don't go making it your fault, either."

"I should have decked him."

"Why, so he could kill you? Stop blaming yourself for everything. I asked for your help on this."

"Don't make it your fault either, Ethel."

"What makes you think I am? Uncle Jack is working with those creeps. Probably they killed Grandpa Jim. And Nestor's momma and daddy made Nestor, so that one's on them. There's plenty of blame to go 'round, Cogbill."

How could I argue with that?

CHAPTER NINE

THE WHOLE WAY home that night I couldn't stop looking for signs of impending doom. Every set of headlights in my rearview was the gaze of the devil himself, or the saucer-eyes of the grim leading the wild hunt. Although intellectually I knew Lazos was not in the backseat, I kept checking the mirror as if a dark shape in a porkpie hat might rise up behind us, jug-eared and grinning, ready to carry us into the pit of the damned.

The long dark drive in the mist, in the midnight shadows of ancient oak and sweet gum did however pass without event, and no set of headlights remained behind us long enough to be of true concern. Nestor's words followed us not only to the house but inside to bed, and hung in the air around us as though he were standing outside every window, grinning with his dead-eyed stare, and I knew with a nauseating certainty that we would never be free of him unless made so by the finality of the grave.

The next day started with the sound of somebody hammering impatiently on my door. I came up out of sleep like a man clawing his way out of the rubble of a collapsed building. Once I was awake, the softness of the blankets and Ethel's skin against my own did not make the task of answering the door any more palatable. I found my pants, and an old baseball bat I had propped beside the bed with Ethel's shotgun.

There were two men on my porch. They were wearing grey suits and skinny neckties, and they were clean-shaven with haircuts as no-nonsense as the plain black Ford in the drive. One was older, his hair the color of gunmetal and his head square, with prominent eyebrows and ears that looked as if they'd gotten bigger with age. There were deep lines under his eyes and from the corners of his nose down the ends of his mouth, into his chin. Despite the fresh shave, his jaws were frosted silver with five o'clock shadow. His shoulders sloped and a gun bulged under the suit jacket, slung below his arm.

The younger man was dark, slighter of build and fresher of face, if no less sober in demeanor. His shoulders were held higher and his holster was worn at his waist. Both had badges identifying them as being from the FBI, but neither of them really needed it.

"Stan," I said. "Ollie."

"I'm Agent Cathy, this is Agent Douglas," said the grey one.

"Cathy?"

"Special Agent Clement Cathy," he said, all business. "But you can call me Agent Cathy. May we come in?"

"Well, I mean...do we have to?"

"Sir?"

"Well it's just that my girlfriend's still asleep and my fox is hungry and he poops when he gets excited. Plus I haven't had my coffee yet and I'm not really done sleeping so if it's all the same, I'd rather not."

"We'll make it plain for you," said Agent Douglas. "Do you know Sergeant Leonard Mahoney, Boston PD?"

"Did he say I did?"

"No sir, we're just following up on an inquiry."

"What's that?"

"We're concerned that you may be interfering with a federal investigation."

"Well, I wouldn't worry about that. Anything the federal government's doing isn't worth my time."

"Say that again."

"I'm fairly sure there's a guy pulling fifty grand whose sole job is flushing tax dollars down a commode," I said. "I spend mine on food and heating oil. I'm probably the idiot. Anyway if we're done here, I'm pretty sleepy. The lady and I had a busy night last night."

"Sir we're not your enemies."

"Thanks for stopping by to tell me that. Y'all have a nice day," I said, and gently closed the door.

In the bedroom I put the bat back with the shotgun. Ethel was sitting up, her hair wild, her big blue eyes staring up at me and a sheet clenched to her breasts.

"Who was that?"

"The FBI."

"Cogbill don't play, it's too early."

"I'm serious." I settled back in to bed and touched her hair. I thought she always looked her best when she first woke up.

"So the FBI's on the case."

"The FBI's on A case. They asked about Len. They started barking up his tree after he made the calls about Drakos."

"So? They're on Drakos, they're on the case."

"Except they're only here because Len called me. They probably annoyed John this morning at the post office. Which means they haven't been watching your uncle's place or they would have seen me by now. It's hard as hell to surveil around Dahlgren, there's no trees and nowhere inconspicuous to leave a car. You'd have to crawl around in the weeds, or go in undercover."

As soon as I said it, I started thinking. I could see Ethel pursuing a similar line of reasoning.

"Could Drakos be an informant?"

"Maybe. But even if that's true, I don't think what's happening in King George is the big thing they're working on. And if it is, they're still going to be more interested in busting the bad guys than protecting your family. Or us."

"Is that why you sent them away?"

"If Nestor thinks I'm talking to the FBI it might endanger your daddy or Jack. Or worse, you. If the FBI is following us around, they're in Nestor's way, and if we're paying their jackass salary they might as well do something useful."

Later, after I'd made breakfast and we'd managed to eat it without Fawkes stealing anything, we washed and dried the dishes together in our usual way.

"How far do we take this? Nestor's threatening your father now. It's only a matter of time until they don't need Jack anymore. They're closing the airport. What happens to him after that might depend on us. The harder we push the harder they'll hit back. What are we willing to risk?"

"So we just let them get away with it?"

"Ethel I'm asking you. You hired me way back at the beginning of all this. It's also your family in danger. I'm asking what you want."

"I told you last night, I don't want to live in fear. I kept thinking I'd wake up and find Lazos standing over the bed. If we don't end this on our terms, we'll be looking over our shoulders forever. Could you live with that, Cogbill?"

"No."

"Neither could I. It would destroy whatever it is we're building here."

"Anything I do from here on out is likely to stir up trouble."

"Well, either I stay here or I go stay with Daddy."

"He's in danger, too."

"Somebody needs to warn him and he don't want to talk to you."

"Will he talk to you?"

"He'll listen to me. And you know he's got a gun."

I couldn't argue with that. We took a shower, dressed, and kissed each other goodbye. The more I thought about it, the more convinced I was that Nestor's threats were largely for dramatic effect. They'd come at me before they went after Ethel or her family.

I needed to take control. I'd been fiddling around wearing cotton gloves and handling everything with tweezers, and hadn't accomplished a damn thing. I should have known better. We didn't liberate Europe with doilies and feather dusters.

As I drove 206, every so often I caught a glimpse of what I hoped was a plain black Ford, just out of sight around the bend behind me on the forest road. At Owens I stopped at the market, no Cadillac in sight, and hung around the hardware while I waited for the other customers to leave. There were only two and although Taylor talked their heads off, they finally made their way back out to the lot and I heard them drive away.

"Taylor, we need to talk."

Taylor reached below the counter and came up with a shotgun.

"You need to get up out of here is what you need to do."

"You gonna shoot me, Taylor?"

"I'll say you tried to rob me."

"I'm not armed. Unless you have a throwdown piece back there you're gonna have a hell of a time explaining to Jay Powell why I'm bleeding all over your hardwood."

His eyes were glassy and I knew he was somewhere else.

"I'll be safer in prison than I will be if I talk to you."

"You'll never be safe, Taylor. What do you think happens when they close that airport? Supply line shuts down and whatever you're doing for them is over. Do you really think they'll be comfortable with loose ends dangling?"

"Cain't get me in jail."

"Don't be stupid. You know what kind of men these are. You think they don't have people inside, even down in Richmond? They'll shank you in the yard or in the shower and sleep like a baby."

I was getting through to him. I could see it. The gun was sagging, there was doubt in his eyes.

"Now if you're willing to punk for some monster who'll fight your battles for you, maybe you'll make it, at least for a while. Could you look yourself in the mirror knowing you gave up your manhood for an extra six months of life in hell? With breasts tattooed on your back and no respect from inmates and guards alike? Is that really who you are? A moral and physical coward with all the personality of a nightcrawler?"

"I shoot you, I call Jimmie. He'll make it go away."

"You shoot me and the two federal agents in the black Ford parked over at Oakland Baptist will come charging in here and make you disappear for interfering with a federal investigation."

"You're lying."

"Look outside. They came to my house this morning, Taylor. They're a little cross because they're investigating your friends and I'm mucking things up. You want to know what I think? I think Drakos is selling out Jimmie Vasiliou."

I could see the frantic wheels turning behind Taylor's eyes.

"I think he's a snitch, and I think you're probably already sunk. But maybe not. Maybe Jimmie really can protect you. If it isn't already too late."

"Get out of here, Cogbill. Leave before I change my mind."

I got back in my car and turned up Owens Drive toward Hud Avery's place. A plain black Ford continued past on Owens Drive after I turned off into Avery's. A big chocolate lab came bounding toward my car, his bark deep and resonant. When he caught me, he turned and trotted beside the car in the cloud of dust as I approached Cloverdale house where it sat perched on the hill. Hud Avery came up the hill in his tractor, the fields spreading below the ridge, several black-and-white cows and a black bull standing around stupidly in the pasture, chewing cud and defecating. I never owned cattle but near as I can tell, this has been their daily routine since Eden.

I heard Avery yell "Buck!" and the dog, tongue and ears flapping, made a hard turn away from the car and off toward his master, looking back at me and throwing the occasional bark my way as he went. The view of the bridge, the water-towers on base, the velocity towers out on the main range, and the intersection below us was even more spectacular by day. Down at Pope's field, bulldozers were tearing up the main runway at the end near 301, exposing the orange clay. I wondered briefly if Jack Pope was still involved, now that his airport was gone and the land was no longer his.

Avery was somewhere between fifty and a hundred years old. His hair was grey, his skin was tanned, and his features looked as if someone had attempted to reproduce an Easter Island statue using exclusively old shoe leather. He was tall and strong, and he wore a plaid shirt with the sleeves rolled to his elbows, the open collar exposing a white t-shirt beneath. His khaki work pants were tucked into a pair of cowboy boots and a big straw Stetson was screwed down on his head.

"What you want, son?"

Buck the dog was jumping around and making soft harrumphing noises.

"You Hud Avery?"

"I didn't catch your name."

"Harry Cogbill. I'm a friend of Ethel Burkitt."

"I know Miss Ethel and her daddy, too. Get down, Buck."

"I guess I'm mostly friends with Ethel."

"Little young for you, ain't she?"

"She's old enough to decide that for herself."

"Frank must love you, partner."

"Frank's okay."

"No he's not, but we'll let that rest. Ethel and her cousins used to come sledding up here in winter. Could walk up from Jim's place down yonder."

"That's why I'm here, actually."

"Ain't much sledding in September, Mr. Cogbill. Come back in February or March. God damn it, Buck." He picked up a big stick and threw it as far as he could, and the dog took off like he'd been shot out of a cannon.

"I was referring to Jim Pope's place. I was wondering if you knew Mr. Vasiliou or Mr. Drakos."

"Prob'ly best you stay away from them men, Mr. Cogbill."

"So that's a yes."

"You ought to be on your way now. Stay away from Frank and Ethel, too."

"I think you've misunderstood me, Mr. Avery."

Buck came back with the stick in his jaws and banged it into Avery's legs. Avery took the stick and held it out at his side, Buck harrumphing after it.

"I asked you to leave."

"I'm trying to help Ethel save her Uncle Jack."

"Repeat that."

"Jack's in trouble. I think Nestor Lazos killed Jim. Either Jack doesn't know or Vasiliou and Drakos talked him into helping cover it up. They have some kind of business relationship. I was hoping you could tell me anything about that path up from the runway to your farm road."

"You a cop?"

"Nope."

He heaved the stick out over the ridge and we watched it sail down into the pasture, the dog blasting out into space and across the field after it.

"I give 'em that piece of land. It's wide at the runway end and narrow down to a little passage just wide enough to drive a truck between the trees and out onto my road. In return they give me a little patch down next to Reed's on 206."

"Why?"

"So I don't have to go all the way out Owens Drive if I don't want to."

"I meant why did they need to make the change. You'd have let them drive across your land if they asked, right? They'd let you drive across theirs, wouldn't they? Either way they still have to use your road."

"Look, I don't ask questions. The Popes always been good neighbors. I flew with Jim. But ever since we traded land, and I give them use of my road, these guys, Vasiliou and Drakos, they're in and out every few weeks. There's a truck the Popes own, an old REO, comes up here from time to time. I don't know what they're hauling, or what they're flying in and out of here. I don't want to know. Vasiliou and Drakos are rude, they leave garbage everywhere they go, and that Frankenstein in the hat..."

Buck came back again, dropped the stick at Avery's feet, and laid down.

"He's a professional killer."

"Frank and Ethel in much danger?"

"We all are."

"You call the Sheriff?"

"We've spoken. He needs evidence and I don't have any. There's no way to prove Jim was murdered unless a witness comes forward. I have nothing to press charges against them for. All it'll do is make them mad. The FBI is watching the Greeks, and matter of fact they're probably parked out on the road now, waiting for me to leave, or do something they can arrest me for."

Avery seemed to consider everything I said. I liked him. At length he said, "what do you want from me?"

"Nothing much. Just keep an eye out. You do business with Owens market?"

"Sure."

"I think it's part of the supply chain. They're moving stuff from the runway, across your land and down to Owens. Or the other way, or both. Don't talk to Taylor about it, he's in it and he's coming apart. But if you see anything, let me know. Do you have a telephone?"

"Sure do."

"Call John at the Gera store, leave a message for me. If it's urgent, call the Sheriff."

"I can handle that."

"Thanks Avery."

He had a peculiar look on his face, like he was considering what he was about to say.

"What's on your mind?"

"I think you should talk to Eli Taylor. No relation to Bob. He rides with a fella delivers produce and meat from some of the farms, to the stores around here. Including Owens Market. If there's something going on, old Eli might have seen it."

"Will he talk to me?"

"Probably. Whatever's going on, I guarantee he's not in it. Got too much pride to risk his reputation like that. Anyone works as many jobs as he does has got to be honest."

"Where can I find him?"

"Up the road a piece, before you get to Hooes. He'll be home about now."

"Thanks Avery. I owe you one."

I turned the car around in front of the big house with the chimney and back out the dirt road to Owens Drive. I went right, toward Hooes, and drove until I saw a little clapboard house on a block foundation, sort of a sad pile, with a tin roof and a chimney puffing thick grey smoke into the air. The porch, the roofline, the clapboard, even the windows and doors – none of the angles were plumb or straight and everything was out of true. It sagged in the middle and listed to the left. The tin roof was rusted red and purple and most of the whitewash was blasted off the siding, leaving a dark grey, huddled shape in a field, a little back from the road. An old pickup was parked in front.

I sat for a moment in the car, watching the smoke rolling out of the stovepipe chimney, and the smell carried me back to December of forty-four. The cold in Ardennes was like something from a long-forgotten epoch. It was impossible to get warm. The Germans were done, and they knew it, and they made one last desperate attempt to turn the tide. They thought they could cut us off from the port of Antwerp and take control, to box us in. Hitler hoped to force a treaty in his favor.

The allied forces were trying to put ourselves back together. This was late in the war and the army had been ground up pretty bad. Most of us at Ardennes were new and had never seen combat. The others were weary, and rough. The black guys were sent to build our numbers back up. They were usually supply men and ambulance drivers. But there were exceptions. There were black artillery units, black infantrymen. Tankers. Their enlistment numbers had surged, I guess there was an appeal in fighting racists on the global stage. They fought bravely, and if not for them the outcome might have been very different.

Now here I was, sitting in my car in front of the home of a man named Taylor. I didn't know Eli Taylor, but I wondered if Eli could be short for Elijah. If so, I was somewhere I had told myself for years that I would never go. I guess the time comes when a man must absolve himself of his past.

I got out of the car as an old woman came in from the field with a basket of green and yellow squash propped on her hip. She set it on the porch and spoke softly to me. Despite her age she was strong, and vital, and her arms were corded with muscle beneath her dark skin. Her head was covered with an old straw fedora, tied down with a scarf, and she was wearing a wash-faded work dress. Her face was round and black, the skin soft, the eyes kind, her lips covered with vertical creases that smoothed out when she smiled.

"Can I he'p you?"

"Mrs. Taylor?"

"Is you here from the bank?"

"No ma'am."

"If you sellin' we ain't buying."

"No ma'am, I was hoping to speak to your husband."

"Well if you ain't taking and you ain't selling I guess it be alright. Wait here."

She stepped up on the porch. The door dragged a little when she pushed it open. The sound of Hank Williams singing "Move it on Over" drifted out the open door.

"Taylor! It's a white man outside."

"Tell him we already done paid."

"He ain't from the bank. He ain't selling neither."

"Gotdammit, I got to get up out my chair."

She turned back to me and smiled. "He work all night, come home work some more. We ain't young no more. It don't get no easier."

"No ma'am. I'm forty and already I have seen evidence of that."

Elijah Taylor was tall and thin, his skin a rich, deep ebony, his hair grown long, straightened and combed into a neat part. It stuck out a bit in back where he'd been resting his head. His jaw was hard and narrow, and his fingertips were worn flat from years of manual labor, and stained with nicotine. He was old, but strong, and veined muscles moved in his forearm when he shook my hand.

There was no question that he was my friend's father. In the large, expressive eyes above high Indian cheekbones, I could see the man PFC Roland Evelyn Taylor might have become had he not thrown himself on the grenade. I could hear Rollie's laugh and see his broad smile as he talked about home. Mr. Taylor stocked shelves at the commissary on base overnight, and in the morning harvested blue crabs from the pots he left in the Potomac near the beacon at Lower Cedar Point.

His wife Iris collected eggs from the chicken coop and tomatoes, beans, and squash from the vegetable gardens in the field behind their house. She washed and mended the clothes, and such necessities as could not be farmed or caught, they traded for or bought on credit at the little country store up the road.

"I was wondering if you'd mind I asked you a couple questions."

Elijah Taylor studied me a moment, his hands pressed to his lower back. He was wearing khakis and a strap undershirt, and a pair of slippers over his socks. Iris picked up the basket of squash and disappeared into the house. They were exactly as I imagined them, and I stood ashamed of the price my ineptitude had demanded of them.

"You a cop?"

"No sir. I'm a friend of Hud Avery's, he said you might be able to help me."

"If you come for eggs you already done missed for the day."

"No sir, although I might take you up on that another time. Avery said you ride along with a farm truck around here sometimes."

"That's so."

"Well, I think there are some bad guys doing business out of the airport down the hill, and I think Bob at Owens Market might know something about it, but he isn't talking. I think he's involved."

"You sure you not a cop?"

"My girlfriend is related to the Popes, she's worried about what they're into and I told her I'd try to sort it out."

"So you doin' po-lice work for free?" He laughed and shook his head. "Girl got ya head turnt around ain't she?"

"Well I'm not complaining."

He laughed some more and smoothed his hair down with a hand.

"That's how it go. Yes sir."

"I guess it is. You ever get a look at what these guys are moving in our out of the store?"

"Mostly try to keep my nose out white folks' business."

"I understand. But if you did see something, it might save some innocent lives."

"Girl even got you talkin' like a cop."

"Right woman'll make a fella feel invincible."

"She damn sure will. I see anything, you keep my name out this business?"

"Absolutely. I'm trying to save lives here."

"Well, maybe sometimes there be a couple crates marked US Navy. Maybe sometimes there be something else. Wadn't no damn oregano or no flour, neither."

"You saw this in the Owens Market?"

"Maybe other places too."

"In the truck?"

He shrugged.

"Does the guy you work with ever make deliveries on base?"

"Yes sir. He do."

"Could you tell me his name?"

"No sir. I don't reckon I will."

"It might save lives."

"Muckin' with them men don't save no lives. I got a family too, sir."

"I understand. Thank you for your time, Mr. Taylor."

Iris reappeared on the porch. She said, "I cain't shake the feeling I seen you before."

"It's possible," I said. "It's a small town."

"That ain't it. What you say your name is, sir?"

I hadn't.

"My name's Harry Cogbill."

"You was in the Army! I seen you in Rollie's pictures."

"Yes ma'am. I'm a friend of your son."

Elijah Taylor's mouth tightened into a straight line, and his face looked like it had been carved out of the side of a mountain.

"Would you come in for a cup of coffee?"

"I'm not sure I should, ma'am."

"Cogbill, get in the gotdamn house."

"Yes, sir."

Mrs. Taylor poured me a cup of coffee. We sat at the kitchen table.

"You scared of black folks, Mr. Cogbill?"

"No sir. Rollie was my friend."

"But you ain't mind standing on my porch acting like you don't know where you is. Been a long-ass time, ain't it, sir?"

"Please, you can call me Harry."

Elijah Taylor fixed his sharp eyes on me.

"How I'm 'posed to call you by your first name you ain't even want to set foot in my house? Quit trynna act like you think we equals. Rollie tell you why he signed up?"

"Said he couldn't fight hate on one front and not the other."

"You know what they give us when he died? A flag. All folt up nice and neat. A flag from a country never showed me a gotdamn thing. And a letter from a president never laid eyes on my boy in his life. A boy who couldn't even vote for him but could damn sure still die in his war."

"He was a brave man."

"You ain't got to tell me."

"He saved my life."

"You got any children, sir?"

"No. I'm not a sir, either."

"It change things. You want to make a better world so they don't got to go through what you went through. Maybe that don't land wit' you. How many times a day you 'fraid for your life?"

"More lately than usual. Usually none."

"Maybe you cain't understand. Let me tell you how brave my boy was. When the army took him, they put him in a all-black unit. Away from the white folks. They sign up to fight and the army ain't trust they ass. They make the black men work harder. Call 'em monkey. Call 'em nigger. Always drew latrine duty. Sometimes one of the white boys shit all over the seat so the niggers have to clean it up. My son had to wait until the last minute to even get a rifle. In the gotdamn United States Army! And when they integrate some of the units at the end the war, and e'rebody fought and bled all over the same ground, what happened? Say it."

"Nobody back home talked about it."

"Rollie wrote us 'bout you, Mr. Cogbill. Said you respect him. That right?"

"Yes sir. I'd say so."

"So why it took you almost fifteen years to come here? My house ain't good enough for you?"

"No, sir. I'm not sure I'm good enough for your house."

"Man, don't give me that. How Rollie gone give his life for yours, and here you is trynna give it back. I cain't undo it. Jesus knows I would. You respect my son, take what he give you and do something wit' it. Damn fool make me get the fuck out my chair. Mrs. Taylor show you out."

I left feeling like a selfish idiot. Perhaps I had not properly honored my friend. It was possible that I had spent too much time alone over the years. It had cost me some valuable perspective. I'd forgotten how to see beyond myself, and my own fears and insecurities, and consider the needs of others. I liked the Taylors, and if I hadn't mishandled the entire situation, we might have been friends. Maybe I could fix it. Ethel would know how.

I grabbed lunch at the Potomac Grill and did not see any sign of Vasiliou, Drakos, or Nestor Lazos. Then I drove down to the wayside, took off my shirt, and sat on the pebbly, shell-filled riverbank and watched the sailboats in the channel, and listened to the sound of the traffic above me on the Morgantown bridge. I thought of Ethel and the way she made me feel; the way my life had changed in the last week because of her presence in it.

In half a day I had already become lonely for her. Mothers watched children splashing in the shallows, men in hip-waders fished a hundred yards out, and as I watched all of this I felt wistful. These were simple pleasures that had been denied me well beyond the age that most men experienced them. I wondered how many of them really understood the enormity of their fortune.

CHAPTER TEN

I GOT BACK into my shirt as I walked up the hill toward the parking lot at the Wayside, and saw them leaning against my car, their trouser cuffs rippling in the breeze: Agent Cathy and Agent Douglas. Douglas was wearing a pair of Ray-Bans. He had his jacket off, his tie loosened, hands in his pants pockets. Cathy was all business, coat and tie still in place, his heavy grey brows casting deep shadows over his eyes.

"Clem and I really need to talk to you, Mr. Cogbill."

"Is it interfering with an investigation if I'm relaxing at a public beach?"

"No, but not talking to us might be."

"I don't have anything to say."

"Well we do, Mr. Cogbill." It was Cathy who spoke this time. "So you can either come peacefully or we can detain you, and I'm past caring which way it goes. You deal the play."

"Fine, let's get this over with."

"Let's take a ride."

I let them lead me to their plain black Ford, and they put me in the front seat, beside Douglas. Cathy sat behind me, where he could keep an eye on me. He was the first to speak after the car pulled out of the lot.

"I probably don't know anything you two aren't already aware of."

"Let us make that determination."

"Right, the government's always got my best interests at heart."

Cathy said, "are you a communist, Mr. Cogbill?"

"Pull this car over right now."

"You don't give the orders here, Cogbill."

"No, but if you're going to insult me, we need to step outside."

"You need to tone it down, sir."

"What did you think was going to happen when you accuse me of being a smooth-brained commie?"

Douglas said, "We made some calls, Mr. Cogbill. You were in the Army, is that right?"

"Yes."

"Got in a lot of fights with your fellow soldiers."

"A few."

"Didn't follow orders."

"Did you have a point?"

"Dishonorable discharge. Series of jobs, didn't last long at any of them."

"You guys really know how to make a fellow feel good about himself."

"Do you know Stavros Balaban?" Cathy said.

"I worked for him for a little while."

"Dimitrios 'Jimmie' Vasiliou?"

"What is this?"

"What do you know about Jerry Drakos?"

"How did he get Jerry out of Nikolaos?"

"He didn't. Jerry is Nicky's brother."

"I didn't know Drakos had a brother."

"They're both in real estate. They sometimes do business under each other's names."

"They're twins?"

"They're idiots."

"What's your interest in Drakos?" Douglas said.

"Do you see the construction site down here on the right, behind the filling station?"

"Sure."

"That used to be an airport belonged to my girlfriend's uncle. He sold it to a company run by Drakos and Vasiliou."

"Let me guess, Drakos bought it, and shuffled it around through a series of shell companies to inflate the value."

"I'm not sure. It isn't that far along yet. They kept the airport open for a few years, but they're up to something. They had a smuggling operation going."

"Nicky Drakos isn't a smuggler."

"What about Vasiliou?"

"Jimmie Vasiliou is the guy Nicky Drakos wishes he could be."

"There were drugs moving through the airport, and the little store I stopped at this morning, next to the church, was part of the supply chain."

"There are other factors involved. Things you don't know," Douglas said.

"Things you don't need to know."

"We're looking at the bigger picture."

"I think it's possible something was making its way off the Navy base, too," I said.

"That would be the Navy's problem. We can't get involved."

"There's a guy named Nestor Lazos in the picture, too. He's made some threats against my girlfriend's family. We just want these people out of our lives."

"Look, Cogbill, you're not a law officer or a licensed investigator. I'm going to give you a friendly warning: stay away from Nestor Lazos. Whatever's going on in this hodunk town isn't worth your life."

"What about hers?"

"Just leave it alone and nobody gets hurt. Vasiliou is too smart to make that kind of a mess. If you push them, they'll come for you. So don't push them. Leave this stuff to the professionals."

They kicked me loose back at Wayside Park. I was full of anger and resentment, burning like bile in my throat. I didn't give a damn about drugs or guns or anything else. People always want what they aren't allowed to have. That's the trouble with rules. People break them. When people want something, that's called demand. Guys who have a supply of the stuff they want, or can make it, will be happy to sell to them. Making it illegal just creates a black market. Guys like Vasiliou only exist because we create the conditions that sustain them. Demand will be answered no matter what.

All I cared about was Ethel Burkitt. I cared about the fact that a lizard named Nestor Lazos might be anywhere near her, and the government that people think exists to protect us couldn't even see us or be asked to muster up a damn to give.

I took 206 to Indiantown Road, and came out on Route 3 near Clift's Garage and the two churches, St. John's and Trinity. The Sheriff's office was in the courthouse. Before they added the wings, Sam Dishman had kept his office in the jury room, and had to vacate when court was in session, but those days were long gone. Sheriff Powell was out and I had to wait a while.

I felt awkward loitering around the courthouse. That seemed like a job for attorneys and people under indictment, and nobody was going to mistake me for an attorney. I wondered if Laurel and Hardy were parked at the Morris's store, or over at Trinity Church or the post office next door. Finally Powell came in, saw me in the hall and looked me up and down.

"Mister Cogbill. Come to confess to burglarizing the motel?"

"I already told you what happened up there, Powell. I came to ask for your help."

"Well, this ought to be good. Come on."

We went into his office, a cold cinder block room with a filing cabinet, a desk and a telephone. There was a rolodex and a jar of pencils, and an oscillating fan on top of the filing cabinet. He took off his hat and smoothed his hair. There was a coat tree that the hat went on, and his jacket, and he pointed me toward a chair in front of his desk and he sat down behind it.

"All right. Shoot."

"I want you to call the staties or maybe the Feds and ask them about a man named Nestor Lazos."

"What the hell for?"

"He's probably what they call a button man. They know him up in Baltimore, DC, and Philadelphia. The FBI is aware of him. I believe he's a sadist who likes to hurt animals. He threatened harm to Frank Burkitt."

"You heard him say he wanted to hurt Frank?"

"It was more of an implication. We were at the Beach."

"Slow down. You were at the beach with this Lazos guy?"

"What? Christ no, I was with Ethel. At Reno Pier in Colonial Beach."

"That's an incorporated town, Cogbill. It's also in the next county."

"But Frank and Lazos are in this county, Sheriff."

"I seem to recall telling you not to leave King George."

"I didn't stay there, did I? Lazos said that Jack Pope didn't care about Frank."

"Now hold on, how in Christ did we get to Jack? You're not going to tell me you think Jack hired this Lazos guy?"

"No, Sheriff, it's the other way around. The Greeks are using Jack. They probably killed Jim."

"Jim Pope was an accidental shooting."

"Accidental shooting?"

"That's right."

"Not a heart attack?"

"Who told you that?" Sheriff Jay Powell smoothed his hair again, then moved the jar of pencils on his desk and put it back in the same spot. "Look I don't want to talk out of turn. Maybe they wanted to spare Miss Ethel of the image. I was Dishman's deputy, I was there. Wadn't no question about it."

"Believe me, Sheriff, I have questions."

"I'll grant there was some confusion at first. When Vashti called Sam, she said her husband had been shot. She was hysterical and wadn't making a lot of sense, so Sam called me, like he did when he thought he might need backup.

"We got out to the Pope place about half an hour later, the doctor was on the way, but when we got there Vashti had been sedated or had done passed out. Any event was Jack we talked to, said old Jim was cleaning his gun, must've not have known it was loaded. Went off and killed him. Terrible thing but wadn't nothing to be done. Doctor got there late, did confirm that Jim Pope was dead from being shot through the head. Didn't take a doctor to know it neither."

"Did Jim Pope own a gun?"

"Most people around here do."

"But did Jim?"

"I don't much appreciate what you're implying. Old Dishman prided himself that there wadn't no violent crime in the county in all his years as Sheriff."

"Well, none that he knew of."

"He was one man. In the early days you could drive for miles and not see a soul. Shoot, most of the county you still can."

"I get it, times were different in Dishman's day. But we're talking about three years ago."

"This idn't Chicago in 1929, Cogbill, let it go."

I couldn't. All I could think about was Ethel, and her family, and how much it would hurt her if anything happened to them. I was looking for help from a small-town sheriff who was mainly used to handling trespassers and domestic disputes.

"Powell, you know this smells funny. You don't think it deserves another look?"

"What the hell is there to do? Jack and Vashti was the only witnesses. Jack give his statement that night. Vashti ain't never come forward but that's her choice. Who am I supposed to interrogate? The widow or the son? Why? I got no evidence of wrongdoing. Let the dead lie."

"These are bad men, Sheriff."

"Then don't piss down their leg. I'm a lawman, Cogbill, I got rules."

"I've got ten," I said. "Moses brought them down the mountain a long time ago, and to tell you the truth I'm a little fuzzy on the back five."

"Boy you're strung tighter than a fiddle, ain't you?"

"What the hell am I supposed to do? I'm telling you about bad guys in your back yard and you won't get off your ass."

"Don't come in here and start swearing at me."

"Or what?"

"Have you been drinking?"

"I don't drink."

"You might consider it."

"Bob Taylor threatened to kill me. I think the Greeks were using his store as a transfer station in a smuggling operation. Nobody would pay attention to trucks coming in and out of there."

"Back up. Bob Taylor threatened you?"

"I went to talk to him."

"He threw you out and you wouldn't leave, is that it?"

"Sheriff."

"It's private property, if you ain't leave when you're asked, that's trespassing."

"A delivery man saw drugs in back of the store."

"Who's that?"

"I promised I'd keep his name out of it. He's a farmer and a waterman, and he rides along with a delivery driver on a farm truck."

Powell ran his hands over his face.

"You're not making a lick of sense. Why don't you start over and tell me from the top exactly what happened."

"Get your goddamn dick out of your ear and maybe you'll hear the words coming out of my mouth."

I am not sure when or how it happened, but we were both standing up. The blood was pulsing so hard in my neck it sounded like a washing machine running just behind my ears. The Sheriff studied me intently.

"You have a real problem with authority, Cogbill. Maybe you'd like to spend the night in jail."

"That depends, is there someone in there with a functioning brain?"

That did it. I thought he was going to come over the desk, but he didn't. I spent the night in a narrow cell, on a metal cot, talking to a shirtless black soldier who squatted in the shadows, his dog tags reflecting the dim red glow of his cigarette.

The walls were carved with a couple of limericks, some choice four-letter words, and crude drawings of male and female genitalia. In the corridor an iron kettle sat upon a radiator. I listened to the rain on the roof and watched the lightning flash through the milky glass of the barred window, until all that was left of Rollie was a cloud of cigarette smoke swirling around the ceiling.

While I was busy wrecking everything I touched, Ethel was having a confrontation of her own. Although it has been my custom in this telling to account only my own experience, for the sake of completion I feel I ought to include this portion of Ethel's story as well.

It was mid-morning when Ethel drove over the cattle guard and up the long orange wheel-ruts to the turnaround in front of her daddy's house. She could remember the smell of the kitchen when her mother was alive, baking pies, mopping floors, and scrubbing mud out of jeans on an old washboard until her fingers bled. A decade had passed and the warmth that Alice Pope Burkitt had brought to the house was like a phantom that dwelt in the shadows, lingering in the closets and the dark end of the staircase. If Frank had ever cried for his wife, it was done in private, and Ethel never knew of it.

And Ethel had cried. She had mourned and confided in girlfriends, but her father, like his grief, seemed entirely removed from her. At fourteen she drank, smoked a few cigarettes, went skinny-dipping in the Rappahannock with her friends, and slept with boys. By nineteen she had grown up and learned that she was an island, that her wit and insight were sharper than the sword of Damocles and she needed no one to tell her what she was capable of. Now, in her twenties, the home she had loved felt alien to her.

When she parked the truck in front of the house, Frank was cutting the far field, and did not acknowledge her presence. The field was golden, the trees green and tipped with the first spark of autumn. The Aermotor was brilliant white in the sun, the tail streaked with rust, the words "Chicago, IL" still visible in red upon it if she squinted. This place, which had always been beautiful in her mind, was tainted with a sadness that seemed to dull the colors and numb the spirit. She had not noticed it before, or had grown so accustomed to it that she scarcely had been aware of it.

Ethel marched into the house, went to her room, and changed into a pair of overalls and a work shirt. She got her boots and gloves by the back door and went to work. At noon she made ham sandwiches and lemonade and brought them to the porch to a small table between a couple of chairs where they regularly took their lunch. Frank ate with her as he always did, but did not speak, or acknowledge her in any way.

"How are you feeling, Daddy?"

"The hell kind of question is that?"

"The kind one human being asks another. Have you been getting along?"

"Didn't expect you home."

"Well God damn it, Daddy, I'm still your daughter."

He downed the last of the lemonade, crushed some ice with his molars, wiped his mouth on his sleeve and stepped off the porch.

She collected the plates and glasses and went to carry them inside, but her hands began to tremble and she threw the whole thing at her feet. The plates chipped and the glasses broke, and melting ice ran between the planks.

"No you don't!"

Frank paused briefly at the sound of her voice, but did not turn to face her.

"Franklin Davis Burkitt will you for God's sake say something?"

He stopped again and called back over his shoulder.

"What do you want me to say?"

"Hell I don't know, tell me you love me. Say you missed me, or you're happy to see me. Tell me I'm a bitch and you wished I'd stayed gone. I don't care but for once in your life say *something*."

"Sandwich was good."

The tractor spat a stream of black exhaust out the stack as the motor rumbled to life.

That evening when the shadows grew long and the sky looked like a mural of purple mountain peaks with their foothills awash in flame, Frank put the tractor in the barn and came in for supper. None had been prepared.

"Daddy we need to talk."

"About what?"

"Uncle Jack's in trouble."

"What kind of trouble?"

"Bad trouble. There's gangsters doing business out of the airport. They probably killed Grandpa Jim. Uncle Jack is under duress and you might be in danger."

"What kind of crap has Cogbill filled your head with?"

"You don't get it, Daddy. I hired him to look into this."

"That ain't all he looked into."

She slapped him. The sound was like a gunshot in the big empty house.

"Daddy why do you think I'm home?"

"Knew he'd let you down eventually."

"He hadn't let me down, Daddy. I'm here because I love you both. Because I shouldn't have to choose between you."

Frank shook his head and turned his back to her, stepping into the shadows in the hall.

"He tell you what was in them papers?"

"He said it had to do with his service record."

"He got some colored boy killed in Ardennes. It broke him. Couldn't even shoot a damn Nazi. If he hadn't let you down yet, baby girl, he will. I promise he will."

"Well he wouldn't be the first man in my life do it."

He wheeled on her.

"What the hell's that mean?"

"What do you think it means?"

"When have I not been here for you?"

"You've never been here for me. When Momma died it was like I lost you both. You're a ghost, daddy. You walk around this house and you work the field but you're not here. Did you even give a damn when she died?"

He came stomping up and bent down and put his face in front of hers, and she was afraid he would hit her.

"Don't you ever say that to me again. Do you hear me Ethel? Never say a goddamn thing like that again."

"How do you think I felt, Daddy? I was dying inside, and every day I'd see you, stone-faced and resolute."

"I had to be strong for you."

"Strong for me? Jesus daddy, you didn't cry so neither could I. Where did that leave us? You don't even realize how screwed up we are."

"What do you want from me?"

Disbelief rose in her throat and blossomed into bitter laughter.

"I want you to be happy, Daddy. Go date women, fall in love. Move on, for God's sakes. It's what I'm doing. I just don't want there to be any question that I love you. I'm leaving this house but I am not leaving you. Just promise me that you won't sit here alone feeling sorry for yourself. You're more than this. Or you used to be."

She was in her room, packing her clothes into a trunk, when the rain came. She sat down on her bed and began to cry. Sheet lightning inverted the night, and she thought she saw a lone figure out across the field. Had there been a black car on the road beyond the fences? In the next explosion of white light, the figure was gone, and so was the car.

When dawn came the next day, I had slept very little. What sleep I did get was fitful, and restless, and I dreamed I was back in Ardennes. Explosions thundered and shook the earth, fresh blood steamed in the snow, and grown men cried for their mothers. The pine forest was drenched in the smell of smoke and human waste as I clawed my way among the dead, the faces of black and white men indistinguishable in the cold and the dirt and the soot.

It was mid-morning by the time Powell kicked me loose. I collected my effects and drove home to feed Fawkes. The dream hung in the air around me, the waking world like a thin curtain that separated me from the horror and the guilt of my wartime failures, adrift like the dead beyond the edges of human sight. My heart was pounding and I was soaked with sweat.

It wasn't a long drive from the courthouse, but everything seemed to move slowly, as if the day itself were heavy with moisture. The roads were shiny and black in the damp morning, the sky like steel. All the details seemed out of focus. The grey tree trunks were streaked black with water, and the leaves seemed phosphorescent in the diffuse light.

When I stepped in the door, Fawkes came snuffling up to me, looking for food.

"Morning, pal." I skritched his fuzzy cheeks and dodged the snuffling nose. I gave him a bowl of Purina and made a pot of coffee for myself. I made breakfast and picked at it, and gave the rest to Fawkes. I was struck by the emptiness of the house, with only me and the baby fox to fill it.

I put on a Hank Thompson record and poked around the house a little, cleaning up the messes Fawkes had made in the night, and then I sat on the porch and scanned the treeline, wondering if Lazos was out there. I did not see him, or the FBI, nor Ethel's red truck bouncing up my drive.

More than ever I was aware of my hollow existence, and the life Ethel breathed into it. I thought it unfair to Ethel that so much of my happiness depended on her, and I was sure that I had offered her nothing worthwhile in return. I did not think I would blame Ethel if she chose to stay with her father.

The rain hammered the tin roof and pelted the trees and turned the fields to mire. Grey fog settled across the yard, creating a sense of isolation so complete as to border on the spiritual. I wondered if in antebellum days this land was part of some sprawling plantation worked by weary slaves dressed in rags, and fed on scraps the master deemed unfit for his own table.

If I squinted I could almost see them in the fog, and hear songs of salvation ringing in the heavy air, laced with coded messages of freedom. Too many died without hope. Now, across the south, their descendants risked their lives for the same cause men have bled for throughout history, to live life on their own terms and on their own land, with the people they loved.

It took the entire pot of coffee to get my motor running even in a limited capacity. When finally I showered, shaved, and dressed, and ventured out into the world, it was with a reluctance I thought had been excised from my life. My tires hissed along the wet pavement, the wipers squeaked faintly and smeared the bird droppings on my windshield as I turned toward John's store.

Through the mist in the air and the water on my windshield, I could barely make out a vehicle stopped on the roadside up ahead. I slowed as I approached, and then, when I was maybe thirty yards off, it resolved itself: a red Ford pickup, about ten years old. Ethel's truck. I pulled over, my heart racing, and looked inside. It was empty. Soon my breath was coming in shallow gasps. There were no signs of a struggle, no clues that I could see except a tire track in the weeds by the roadside. I forced myself to breathe slowly, deliberately, but the slushing in my neck was going full-tilt again.

It was inevitable that wherever there was goodness, hope, and joy, the forces of evil would conspire to take them away. If there was one constant in the world I knew, that was it. If the cloud of failure and defeat that followed me back from Europe had now swallowed Ethel, then absolutely nothing was sacred, and all hope merely the setup for despair.

CHAPTER ELEVEN

I SAW no use in going to the sheriff. Perhaps I was being cynical, but I felt that my outbursts and my general disdain for authority had destroyed any chance I had of credibility in his eyes. In any case, if Ethel had not been missing for twenty-four hours she wasn't legally missing, and by law the Sheriff couldn't do much anyway. So I drove out to the Burkitt house and prayed to God Frank would listen to me.

The house looked cold and lonely in the grey, like a ghost ship coming to harbor after a hundred years at sea, colorless and indistinct in the fog and the rain. It called up a memory of my childhood, standing on a pier at Nags Head, North Carolina, a huge ship on the horizon, its lights burning cold in the mist, a phantom shape foreign to my young eyes. I splashed across the orange mud and up onto the porch, hammering on the door.

Frank appeared, his face darkening with disgust at the sight of me.

"What do you want?"

"I've come about Ethel."

"My opinion obviously don't matter to either of you, so I don't know what you're looking for."

"I'm looking for Ethel."

"She ain't with you?"

"When did you last see her?"

"You know good and goddamned well when I seen her last. She does what she wants."

"Her truck's sitting empty out on Gera Road, Frank. I just spent the night in jail, so you'll excuse me if I'm a little behind on current events. When goddammit did you see her last?"

His face went through a series of contortions as I spoke.

"She packed her things and left this morning. Probably she had engine trouble. Did you check with the neighbors?"

"Did she tell you about the Greeks?"

"Are you an alcoholic, Cogbill, or is it something worse you're addicted to?"

"Say that again."

"This ain't Chicago or New York. That gangster shit don't happen out here. I think you left your sense in Ardennes."

He turned his back to me and pushed the door closed behind him as he disappeared into the darkened house. I picked up one of the chairs on the porch and threw it into the lawn, then splashed back to my car and drove away.

I could only think of one or two more plays. Route 206 felt like an endless slog, but finally I saw St. Paul's perched on its hill among the ancient tombstones and the craggy trees, and then Berthaville was behind me and Owens came and went, with its market and Oakland Baptist, and then I hit US 301 and a long mile later the little cinderblock Texaco station on the left. I crunched across the wet gravel and in through the office door to the right of the two service bays. Jack Pope had on a flannel shirt and a pair of jeans. His salt and pepper hair was combed back, the curls tamed since last I'd seen him. He put his hands on his waist and shook his head.

"What in hell are you doing here?"

"They took Ethel."

"What are you talking about?"

"They took Ethel, Jack."

"What did you do?"

"I talked to Bob Taylor."

"The hell did you say to him?"

"I may have suggested that Drakos is an FBI informant."

"That's the stupidest thing I ever heard."

"Taylor didn't think so."

"Bob don't have the sense God give a turnip."

"Are you going to help me or not?"

"I'm going to find out what's going on. I still don't see why they'd take Ethel."

"Because they couldn't get to me. I spent the night in jail."

"Then how do you know they took her?"

"She was staying at Frank's. I guess she left to come back to my place and now her truck's sitting empty on the side of the road."

"Maybe she broke down. Truck's old. Maybe she's setting at your house now wondering where you are."

It was pointless to try and explain. Deep in some animal place, a genetic remainder of Neanderthal man, I knew that Ethel was in danger. I couldn't understand how her family could be so glib about it all. I had the feeling of a sane person trapped in a lunatic asylum. The reverse could also have been true.

"Jack. We're talking about Ethel here."

"Let me make some calls, will you? Be somewhere else for a while."

I stepped outside to look around. Beside the filling station lot, from the road to the near end of the main runway was all just orange mud, rainwater puddling in the tracks left by the bulldozers. A sign was posted nearby showing a map of the projected Cloverdale Subdivision. The two runways would become the main roads, Danube and Delaware Drives.

The section immediately behind the filling station on the south side of Danube was slated for commercial development. An apartment building was to go up on the other side of the street, nestled between 301 and Williams Creek. There was a waste water lagoon to be dug out in the forest near the back of the neighborhood, and a couple of small parks or common areas were planned between some of the cul-de-sacs. Lots were for sale. Phase One was a planned cul-de-sac called Baltic Place, to the right, just beyond the proposed site of the apartment building. There were three models being offered, but construction had not begun.

They didn't need Jack at all anymore, and if they didn't need him, anything could happen to Ethel or Frank or anyone else, just so everyone was quiet. I was the squeaky wheel; if anyone needed greasing in any sense it was me, and I would gladly trade my life to save Ethel's.

"Hey Cogbill!"

Jack's voice knifed through the damp air and out over the creek. I jogged back over to the service station door.

"Jimmie Vasiliou wants to talk with you."

"Okay, put him on."

"Not on the phone, man. Go see him at Wilkerson's. Come alone. You bring anybody else and he's gone."

"I got enough people in the soup already. I'll be alone. Can I ask you a question?"

"Cain't promise I'll have an answer."

"It doesn't bother you, to stand here and look out the door at what's happening to everything your family built?"

"You know how there are moments in our lives that define us, for better or worse?"

"Sure."

"You ever notice it's the wrong ones we get stuck inside of?"

Jack might as well have pierced me with a sword.

At Wilkerson's, there were a couple of Chevys and a green Olds parked in the gravel. There was no Caddy in sight. I put my mackinaw and my hat on the coat tree by the door and sat in back, at the table where Jimmie and his boys had been the night Ethel and I had our dinner date. I put my back to the wall and watched the front door. If Vasiliou or Lazos came in I would see them. If it looked like bad trouble I could run out through the kitchen. That I was thinking like Vasiliou was not lost on me.

There was a man and a woman eating lunch at a table, an older guy at the counter drinking coffee and reading a paper, and a third man who never looked my direction. He finished his coffee, left some bills on his table and walked out. A few moments later Jimmie Vasiliou walked in. He shook the rain off his grey trench coat and hung it, and his fedora, on the coat tree.

He was well-dressed as always, his dark hair slicked down and his painted tie neatly knotted in a full Windsor. A ring glistened on his right hand. He was thick-bodied, broad-shouldered and paunchy. His clean-shaven face was round and full of color as he waddled across the room and sat down.

"You didn't bring Nestor along to pat me down?"

"You're not carrying. And you're no killer."

"What about you?"

"Just a regular businessman."

"Right. Hot-mix asphalt treating you okay?"

"I guess you asked around about me, too."

"A little."

"Let's skip the dick-measuring, it don't impress me. We're men of the world. We both served."

"You were a supply clerk."

"In the Marine Corps, and I can take your skinny grunt ass any day of the week." He smiled when he said it, like we were old friends.

"Okay, you want to cut to the chase. Where's Ethel?"

"I'm afraid I don't know. You have my word that I had nothing to do with her disappearance. All I know is what Mr. Pope told me on the telephone."

"Then why meet with me?"

"Because you're a pain in the neck. Because I hoped to extend an olive branch."

"What about Nestor?"

"What about him?"

"He threatened us."

"I'll be frank with you, Mr. Cogbill. I don't believe all of Nestor's wiring is intact. I wouldn't have hired a guy like that."

"You're going to tell me he isn't an associate of yours?"

"I'm just a broker, Mr. Cogbill. I have friends in Baltimore, businessmen, who put up some money on a residential development. Nicky, now, he's in real estate. He's the one who saw the opportunity here."

"Nicky? You mean Drakos."

"Right. I bring the money and the opportunity together, in return I get a seat on the board, and a slice of the pie. Nothing illegal about any of that, is there? Here's a hint: no there is not."

"And Nestor's the representative for your friends in Baltimore?"

"Not hardly. No, they trust me to be straight with them. Nestor's line of work is more like...security."

"Right."

"He's very good at, ah, security. But like I said, I don't think he's wired right. Unfortunately, I'm saddled with him. So, I apologize for anything he may have said to you or Miss Burkitt. Please understand that his words and actions do not represent me."

"Yeah, you're a regular Eleanor Roosevelt."

"I think you missed your calling as a comedian, Mr. Cogbill. Like that gag you pulled with Mr. Taylor. Nicky's what I call a smart dummy. He always got a plan, a way to make a quick buck, but he's not smart enough to think it through all the way. Yeah he tried some scams in his younger days, it didn't work out well for him, cos he's a smart dummy. But he does have an eye for opportunity. What I'm telling you, there's nothing to fink to Uncle Sam about here. Nicky's a bum but he's not a rat. All we ever did was pay Taylor a fee to borrow some warehouse space. That day you saw us there, we were ending our arrangement. All above board. I've nothing to hide."

"Then why don't you tell me what you were warehousing?"

"Packages. I don't know what was in them. My friends in Baltimore are in the import-export business. They were workshopping a new distribution system but it wasn't practical so they canned it. That's all I can tell you. Only a crook would open up someone else's boxes."

"What's this got to do with Ethel?"

"Nothing, Cogbill. That's the point. I didn't take her. There's no blackmail here, no threat. Why would I risk a legitimate moneymaking venture on a kidnapping?"

"What about Nestor?"

"Nestor's his own man. Anyway, I got my own business to attend to up home. So as much fun as I've had smelling skunk funk and dodging drooling possums, I'm leaving town. Here, let me buy you lunch."

He put some money on the table and got up to leave.

"I recommend the meat loaf."

"I'm not hungry."

"Have it your way."

I followed him outside and saw him get in the passenger side of the green Oldsmobile. The driver may have been the man who had walked out of the diner before Jimmie walked in, but I didn't get a good look at him. They went North, toward the Morgantown Bridge, and the state of Maryland.

I kept hearing the words "Nestor's his own man" over and over again in my head. My shoulders felt like a tightrope and my ears were ringing. I could only think of one more play. I'd been avoiding direct confrontation to keep Ethel out of danger, but now Ethel was in danger. What reason did I have not to kick the hornet's nest?

I skidded out of the parking lot at Wilkerson's, blew gravel all over the place, and raced south to Owens in the hazy grey mess. I nearly collided with another car at the intersection with 206. It was so close the other driver and I looked each other in the eye as we slid past one another in the mist, brakes screaming, tires howling, and then I was up the big hill and in the lot at Hillcrest.

The motel sat up on a slight rise above the parking lot. There were a few small runs of concrete steps at intervals along the grass incline, perpendicular to a narrow sidewalk that ran the length of the red brick lodge. The wooden doors were narrow and white, little more than two feet wide, and a steep step up from the concrete walk.

Nick and Nestor's room was situated just about halfway down. The door was outfitted with a little bronze knocker but I used the meaty part of my fist, thumping impatiently until I heard the bolt turn, and I crashed through like a fullback, shoulder down, driving with my legs. I heard Drakos swear as he stumbled and fell against the dresser and his ass hit the floor.

My palms were sweaty and none of my clothes seemed to fit right. Possibly it was my skin. I clenched and unclenched my fists and kept shifting my weight side to side.

"Jesus Cogbill, what are you doing?"

I kicked the door shut with my heel.

"Where's Ethel Burkitt?"

"I don't know, and I don't care!"

I hauled him up off the floor and slammed him against the wall. His curly hair was disheveled and he needed a shave.

His brown eyes were wide and full of fear. His shirt was the wrong size, too long in the sleeves and too loose in the collar. His necktie was loose and whatever it was made of wasn't silk. His collar was unbuttoned and being a size too large to start with, I could see a ring of grime the color of last week's lemon rinds all around the inside.

"Where's Nestor Lazos?"

"Man I don't know, he don't answer to me."

"Who does he answer to? Jimmie?"

"No man, and I sure as hell ain't gonna tell you who. What the fuck is your beef?"

The pulsing in my neck began again, the sloshing behind my ears, my face stinging as though hot sand were blowing against it. He grabbed my arm and put a hand to my face and tried to push me away from him, fumbled around and poked me in the eye; it was an accident or he'd have had it out. I threw an awkward left into his gut. It was a miserable punch but it caught him in the solar plexus and he huffed a little and his grip loosened, so I pulled my right arm free and got him in the kidney, and when he dropped his arm I popped him in the nose.

The klaxons were going again. I grabbed his grubby collar and just kept hitting him. My hand started to feel like an eggplant but I just didn't care. His nose broke, his lips turned to pulp and the skin split against the bone of his forehead. There was blood all over his shirt and tie, dripping on his shoes and staining the carpet. He was out on his feet. When I let go of him he sagged and slid down to the floor. The back of my hand had inflated so bad I couldn't see my knuckles.

I pulled a brown sock out of his suitcase and used it to cover my hand when I opened the door. I pulled it shut behind me and got out of there. I threw the sock out the car window on 301, and just drove, not knowing where I was or what I was doing. I heard a static-covered voice say "breathe, man," and I went to switch the radio off only to find that it wasn't on to begin with. I thought I smelled cigarettes. I was a mess. There was a sound like windchimes; with a sort of sub-audible whoosh, the fog lifted off my brain and I recognized that I hadn't learned anything from Drakos. My right hand on the shifter looked like a baby's fist writ large, the knuckles just little dimples, the skin smooth and pink. The pain was subsiding, but it would be fat and tender for a week or so.

Drakos wouldn't call the sheriff. If anyone at the motel did, he still wouldn't talk. Regardless of what Jimmie Vasiliou claimed, they all had things to hide. All I could think to do was go home and see if Nestor was there, or if he had left me any threats or ultimatums. Probably I'd never see Ethel again. Love was not meant for me, and no happiness could flourish in my soil. All that was dear to me I always lost.

I would find Nestor Lazos, and kill him, and if I wound up in prison then so be it. Life was a miserable hole of a thing anyway, and there was no greater punishment imaginable than to go on living among the blithe and smiling people, who always got their way and never paid any dues, while the rest of us toiled in factories to make their food and mopped their piss off the floors of public restrooms.

Back on Gera Road, Ethel's truck was no longer anywhere in sight. I went to the store to check my mail, in case there was a note from Lazos or anything else useful.

"Hey there Cogbill, what-say?"

"My mail, John."

"How's Miss Ethel?"

"My mail, John!"

My breath felt short, my neck and shoulders tight, and I didn't quite know what to do with my hands. John brought me my mail, but there was nothing of consequence.

"What you do to your hand?"

"I guess I hurt it."

I left John looking hurt and confused, and drove home in a kind of crackling black energy from which I could see no escape. But my vision was as myopic as it had been all day. I parked the car and sat there for a few minutes in the driveway, choking, shoulders heaving, the totality of my failure crashing down upon me with the weight of the hand of God. At last I dragged my miserable carcass out of the car, up the step onto my drooping gallery, unlocked the door and lurched into my living room.

Ethel Burkitt was on the couch, curled up with Fawkes and a blanket I didn't recognize. She was drinking coffee and reading a book by John Knowles.

"Evenin' Cogbill, where ya been?" Her face changed when she took a proper look at me, and she sat up and put the book and the coffee on the table.

"What happened? Lord, Hieronymus, are you hurt?"

Unable to speak, my legs tumbling bonelessly like the limbs of a scarecrow, I practically fell into her arms. Fawkes sprang up onto the back of the couch, and Ethel put her hands in my hair and locked my eyes with her blue gaze.

"I thought Lazos took you. Your truck..."

"It broke down and I started walking."

"I've been all over, Frank, Jack, Jimmie Vasiliou, and Nick Drakos, I..."

"Freda went driving by and stopped to pick me up. I had to call for a wrecker and got it towed to Clift's. Then I got her to bring me here, only you weren't home, so I been mainly setting around lookin' pretty. Have you been fighting? You're holdin' me so tight you're liable to break something. I mean something of mine, in case I wasn't clear."

I did not let go. I kissed her, and she kissed me back.

"I thought...I'm all messed up. I'm not right. I'm sorry."

She took my hand.

"How did things go with your daddy?"

"Well, he's stubborn and miserable."

"Frank? Never."

"I cain't stand it anymore, Cogbill. I cain't fix him."

"Ethel, it isn't your job."

"The whole time I was at daddy's I kept thinking I couldn't wait to get back home."

"I kept thinking it wasn't home without you."

"Harry Cogbill, I'm here."

I picked her up and carried her to the bedroom. We made love with an urgency that beat back the chill and the colorlessness of the day, and broke the electric blackness around me. I disappeared into her embrace, and emerged whole again. She turned her blue eyes up at me, and I stroked her hair and held her, and for a little while, nothing else mattered but that we were together.

Later, I fixed us something to eat. I had set aside a couple of steaks, marinating in Worcestershire sauce and crusted with black pepper and sugar. I set a large pot of water to boil. While that was going I peeled a few potatoes and dug out a couple of eyes, then chopped them up and put them in the pot to soften. Ethel ran interference on Fawkes while I worked, and I filled her in on what I'd been doing since the morning she left for her daddy's place.

"We'll straighten things out with Mr. and Mrs. Taylor," she said when I told her about my visit. "Why didn't you tell me Rollie was black?"

"I was a different person before the war. When the mortar rounds are going off, the color of the skin on the guy fighting beside you just doesn't seem all that important."

"Reckon that's as it ought to be."

I hadn't thought it was possible to love Ethel any more than I already did.

"I won't repeat to you what some of the guys said after Rollie was killed."

"You aren't a coward."

"I don't mean what they said about me."

The comment hung there a minute, and then Ethel closed her eyes and put her head down.

"That was the end for me. I got in a lot of fights. It got hard to tell who the enemy was anymore. I realized there are no good guys."

"So why help me?"

"Because there ought to be."

I melted some butter in my skillet and then put the steaks on medium heat. While they were going I steamed some green beans, drained the water out of the potatoes, added milk and butter, and mashed them. I left them a little lumpy because I like them that way. I turned the steaks a couple of times until they were blackened on the outside and still a mild pink on the inside.

"Did you go to the sheriff about the man you saw in the field at your daddy's house?"

"I couldn't describe the man I saw. I'm not even sure what kind of car it was, it was far away and I could only see it for a split-second. Maybe it was your FBI guys. Anyway the sheriff didn't seem to feel like he could do anything. He also advised me to keep away from you."

"I note that you have not taken his advice."

"I guess we're both bad at following orders."

CHAPTER TWELVE

AFTER DINNER we did the dishes together, then I put on a Kitty Wells record and Ethel curled up with me on the couch and resumed reading her book. It was a perfect evening and the worry-wrought day was but a distant memory, an episode in another man's life. That my behavior might be unnatural rarely entered my thoughts in those days. When it did I usually found something else to think about.

It was like there were two people living in my skull. One of them dwelt permanently in the valley of the shadow of death, and woke each morning with the horrible knowledge that everything he loved was speeding daily toward the grave, and the best anyone could do was prolong the experience. The other, new since the arrival of Ethel Burkitt in my life, existed always in the moment, frozen in the air above the diving board, weightless in anticipation of the plunge. It was my struggle to reconcile these seemingly irreconcilable beings.

I came up out of my funk at the sound of a knock on the door.

"Take the shotgun, Cogbill. A knock this late ain't never good news."

I did not take the shotgun. I opened the front door and found Jay Powell on my porch.

"Evening, Sheriff."

"Cogbill, you're getting to be a chronic condition. I just come from the Hillcrest. This Nicholas Drakos—"

"Whatever that man told you is a lie."

"He claims he slipped in the shower. The couple next door on the other hand, nice people, down from Jersey on their way to Florida, was them what called it in. Said they heard a lot of yelling and cursing and they thought somebody was fixing to come through the wall."

Ethel had come to the door now and she smiled warmly.

"Hello Sheriff, can I offer you a cup of coffee?"

"No Miss Ethel, thank you. I see you haven't taken my advice."

"Sheriff I don't believe that's any of your business."

"No ma'am, I don't reckon it is."

"Let me know if you change your mind about that coffee."

"This fella from Jersey, he looked out the window and seen a guy in a mackinaw and a fedora jump in a red-on-black Ford – I like your new car, by the way – and take off like his ass were on fire. Now you're not gonna stand there with that club-hand and tell me you didn't do it."

"Do what, jump a guy in the shower? One night in a holding cell and you think it's come to that?"

"Cogbill, you're lucky he ain't pressing charges."

"Am I? If you're so sure about what happened, why do you think he doesn't want to talk to you? What possible reason could he have?"

"Look, I'm sympathetic, I truly am. Miss Ethel talked to me at length today about the man in the field on her daddy's farm. Now I believe you think you're helping. You probably even think you're on the side of the angels. But unless anyone has a crime to accuse these fellas of, all I got is you stirring up shit. Nobody likes a shit-stirrer, Cogbill. Especially sheriffs."

"I'm not under arrest, is what I'm hearing here."

"No, but you're damn sure trying. One more stunt like this and I'll find a reason to lock you up."

"Why don't you talk to Bob Taylor?"

"Don't push me. Goodnight, Miss Ethel."

I watched him turn his car around and roar back down my drive. Ethel and I retired for the evening and only then did I see that she had brought a trunk of her personal belongings with her from her daddy's house. There were extra pillows and an afghan at the foot of the bed. Well, hell. It was still worth it.

The next morning, Ethel wanted pancakes for breakfast. They were not one of my specialties; I have never been fond of them. So she mixed the batter while I started the coffee and got the bacon going, and we moved around the kitchen in a kind of easy, familiar rhythm without getting in each other's way.

After breakfast, we went over to see John and get our mail. The rain had let up and the early sun was already drying out the wet clay and cracking the mud in the tire ruts of my driveway. Gera road was silver and the gravel in the macadam glittered like precious jewels, the moisture still clinging in dark swaths to the cracks along the edges of the road surface. The grass seemed to have grown three inches overnight.

At the store, Ethel borrowed the phone to call Clift's garage and check up on her truck. They expected to have it done by the end of the day. So we bought some ice and went home. I made up a batch of my fettucine alfredo, put it in a casserole dish, and wrapped the chicken breasts in tin foil and put it in an old metal cooler. Then we made sandwiches and packed a thermos of lemonade and a couple of Cokes, put the cooler in the backseat of the car, and drove out to Hooes. Ethel assured me that this was the way people handled such things, but I was busy contemplating half a dozen or so ways it could misfire.

We parked beside the old pickup truck in front of the Taylor house, and got the casserole dish and the package of blackened chicken out of the cooler. Iris Taylor was sitting on the porch shelling peas. She got up when she saw us get out of the car.

"You must be Mrs. Taylor," Ethel said.

"Is you Mrs. Cogbill?"

"Well, we hadn't quite got that far," Ethel said.

"This is Ethel Burkitt, my girlfriend."

"I sure hope what you carrying ain't for us," Mrs. Taylor said.

"Cogbill here felt like kind of a jerk after his visit the other day, and we wanted to apologize to you and your husband."

"Keep this one, Mr. Cogbill, she all right."

"I know it."

"Taylor asleep right now," Iris said. "Got to work tonight. I'll let him know you stopped by. Let me get you some tomatoes and squash from the garden."

"That won't be necessary Mrs. Taylor."

"What Cogbill means to say is, thank you very much and we'd be delighted to have some homegrown veggies."

"Baby girl, you might straighten him out yet."

Iris brought us a cardboard flat that looked as if Elijah had rescued it from the stockroom at the commissary, and she had filled it with a dozen large tomatoes in various stages of ripeness, and several pounds of zucchini and yellow squash.

"You're very generous," I said.

"It all looks delicious," Ethel said.

"I get your casserole dish back in a day or two."

"Maybe you'd like to come over for dinner sometime next week?"

"Oh, now Miss Ethel, that ain't necessary."

"Your son was Hieronymus' friend. We'd very much like the chance to get to know you and your husband. Cogbill's always had such good things to say about Roland. It would mean a lot to us both."

"That right, Mr. Cogbill?"

"Yes ma'am. That's why I brought Ethel, she says these things better than I do. She speaks for us both."

"I talk it over with Taylor. Could I have your address?"

I gave it to her.

"I'll write soon. You got any sense, Cogbill, you put a ring on that girl's finger."

"Yes ma'am."

When we left the Taylor's house we drove out to Wayside Park and ate our sandwiches on the riverbank, drank lemonade and watched the boats in the channel. The sun stitched her light brown curls with copper and gold, and brought out the dusting of freckles across her cheeks. We had worn our swimsuits under our clothes, so after our lunch settled we went out and splashed around in the shallows, and hunted for sharks teeth amidst the pebbles and shell fragments crusting the riverbank, then laid down and dried out in the sun.

I could imagine a future where Ethel and I brought our children here on Sunday afternoons in summer, after church, to swim, and fish, and listen to their squeals of laughter as they played pretend and chased each other around the park. This kind of vision was new to me, after years of living with the specter of death, and it was hard to believe that this could be my life.

Ethel's swimsuit was green with white trim, and had a strap that looped around behind her neck to hold the front up. She had a pair of sunglasses pushed up in her hair, and I admired her legs and her shoulders, and the way she scrunched one eye shut in the sun when she turned to talk to me. I tried to think of some way to tell her how beautiful she was, how every moment I spent in her presence was like a waking dream, but these were mere platitudes and would mean nothing when spoken aloud, regardless of how truly I felt them.

"Cogbill, what's on your mind?"

I couldn't decide what to say, so I just smiled at her.

"Naughty things, huh?"

"No, Ethel."

"Really? You don't like the swimsuit?"

"Of course I do."

"You don't like what's in the swimsuit?"

"Jesus, Ethel."

"When I's about fifteen or sixteen I used to go skinny-dipping in the Rappahannock out on my friend's farm."

"What's that like?"

"Saves on laundry."

"Do that here you're liable to get arrested."

"Well for heaven's sakes, I wasn't about to. I'm just tryin' to figure out what's on your mind."

"Everything."

"Well if you don't want to tell me."

I put my arm around her waist and pulled her close, then put my other hand behind her head and put my face beside hers.

"You're everything, Ethel."

She put her arms around my neck and stroked my hair.

"Well, now you tell me."

By this time it was getting into the late afternoon, so we packed up our things and drove back to Gera. I had been unburdened of a measure of the weight I had carried for half my life. The feeling was such a relief that there was a lightness to my spirit that I hadn't felt since probably before the war, perhaps as far back as childhood, when my biggest concerns were bicycle tires and chewing gum. It was easy to believe, if I didn't think too hard about my still-swollen hand, that Ethel and I were free from the evil that had introduced itself into our lives. But before the evening was out, it was to come roaring back.

Back at the house, we showered together, and did some other things, and then we put on fresh clothes and I took Ethel over to Clift's to pick up her truck. Paying for the repair would have used up the last of her money, but they knew her and said they'd bill her, and she could pay later. I had to find a job, and soon, and I'd feel better about that when I knew we were out of danger and our gangster troubles resolved.

"You go on home," I told Ethel. "I've got to end our problems with Lazos. The only way out is through."

"Cogbill, what are you going to do?"

"Everybody's being so careful. Bad guys trying to avoid the law, law officers following rules, me trying to protect you...I'm the one keeps getting in trouble."

"I noticed."

"Because I'm the only one not trying to cover his own ass. I've got to go see Drakos again."

"You know what the Sheriff said."

"He hasn't arrested me yet."

"Do what you got to do. Fawkes and I'll still be here."

I made it to the bank just before they closed. In a safe deposit box, I had a light brown lockbox containing a Remington 1911, my sidearm from my Army days. I was never sure why I couldn't bring myself to pawn the thing, but I always felt compelled to keep it someplace inconvenient, so I wouldn't get it out unless I really needed it.

I retrieved the lockbox and took it out to my car, then checked everything out. Inside the box the gun was wrapped in a cloth and there was a magazine and a box of .45 caliber ammunition. I'd cleaned and oiled the piece before I put it in there, and it was in good condition. I loaded it and put it in my coat pocket, then drove to Hillcrest.

I knew the real problem was Lazos, but the only way I had to get to him was Drakos. Nicky wasn't a tough guy, and what I'd done to him when I thought they'd taken Ethel was hardly a badge of honor. Could I kill either of them? In self-defense, yes. But could I make it necessary to defend myself? Well, why not? By now there was hardly a human being on the planet I hadn't pissed off.

It was getting dark, and sheet lightning blasted the sky away above the treetops ahead of me as I drove, somewhere over the Potomac. The car almost bottomed out on the dip pulling into the Hillcrest lot as the rain began to fall. It came all at once, hard and strong, and ran in waves down my car windows. There was no Cadillac in sight. I stepped up and knocked calmly on the green door.

"Who's there?"

"It's Cogbill, I come to apologize."

"Cogbill? Jesus man, once ain't enough? I ain't said anything to the Sheriff, okay, so you ain't in no trouble. Just take it easy."

"I'm calm, Nicky. I mean it, I came to apologize."

The door opened. Drakos had cotton wadded up his nose and an ice pack pressed to his head. His lips were swollen, and he had a bandage on his forehead.

"You're supposed to be home, Cogbill."

"What's that mean?"

I pushed past him into the rustic little motel room.

"I got nothing to say to you, man."

"That's not what Jimmie told me."

"What the hell are you talking about?"

"I wasn't in a good place, but I did get to talk to Jimmie before he left. If that guy's your friend you've got it worse than I do."

"Jimmie said something about me?"

"Yeah, well, you know how he is. He only looks out for himself."

"What did he tell you?"

"He said you're an idiot and an easy mark. He said this whole thing was a mess and he was leaving it in your lap. If I were you I'd be looking over my shoulder. You got enough problems without me adding to them."

"He didn't say that."

"He said if Nestor took your head off it wouldn't lower your IQ."

"You're talking out your ass, buddy. I'm in real estate."

"Okay, maybe it was me that said it. Whose money are you playing with?"

"I hadn't done nothing wrong."

"What about Jim Pope?"

"I didn't have nothing to do with that."

I smiled.

"You're wasting your time, Cogbill. All I want is to get out of this mudhole and back to Washington. You should go home."

"You guys are a cancer. Not just on this town but on everything you touch."

"You ain't exactly King Midas yourself, man."

I took out my gun and pointed it at him.

"We can do this the easy way or the hard way. Give me Nestor."

"Whoa, whoa, what the shit are you doing?"

"What I should have done a long time ago."

"You ain't a killer, Cogbill, come on. Jimmie showed us your Army record, you ain't got it in you."

"There are no good guys, Nicky. The world's a mudhole. Guys like you keep adding water. Somebody's got to shut it off before the rest of us drown."

"Man, you want to kill me? You ain't thought that through, have you?"

"Let's take a ride, Nicky."

"No way in hell, Cogbill. You want to kill me, you're gonna have to do it in this shitty motel where all the neighbors can hear. Go ahead, prove you're man enough."

"Where's Nestor?"

"Oh, Jesus, that's gold." Drakos pulled a piece of cotton out of his nose and dropped it on the carpet. "You ain't listening to me, are you? You're supposed to be home. Christ, you're almost as sick as he is."

There was a sound like a man sucking spit off his lips just beside my ear, but there was nobody there. My heart was pounding so hard I thought my ribcage would explode. I ran out of the room and into the rain, my failure complete, a monument to my ineptitude.

Ethel found she couldn't get settled. She fed Fawkes, and made a sandwich for herself. She read the same paragraph of John Knowles about three times, then fussed around the house a while. She started to undress for bed, then changed her mind. She could not shake the feeling of being watched. She put on another pot of coffee and tried Knowles again.

The porch creaked, and Ethel got up and opened the door to find Nestor Lazos, the rain dripping off his porkpie hat, spattering the lapels of his trench coat. He was wearing gloves, and a dark grin of the kind she had always associated with Caligula.

"Yo, Miss Burkitt. You ain't had to keep your clothes on, on my account."

The hair on her arms and on the back of her neck stood up, the violation of her privacy like a fist to the gut. She tried to slam the door but he put his foot in and held it there. She stomped on it, but she was in her socks and he had on oxfords and rubber overshoes.

"You make me want to shower in bleach, Nestor. Were you born in a hospital or did they find you in a Dempster-dumpster?"

"You got a mouth on you. Does Cogbill like your mouth? I bet he do."

"The sheriff is on his way."

"Sure."

"You need to leave. When he gets here he'll arrest you."

"I won't be long. I need to have a brief discussion with your fella about the way he remodeled Nicky's face. He takin' a dump or something?"

"I think I hear the sirens now, Nestor."

"He's not home. His car ain't here. Daddy gone and left you all alone."

"Cogbill'll be along shortly. That thing he did to your buddy's face? Well, you're next, mister."

She heard him sniff with amusement.

"I thought in the southern parts of the country it was customary to offer a guest a cold glass of lemonade, or perhaps sweet tea."

"You cain't hurt me, you promised Uncle Jack."

"So much for southern hospitality."

He shoved the door in, and she stumbled as she turned to run.

My wipers were scraping across the windshield as I sped down 206, lights on porches and in windows shattered into fractal images by the fine droplets on my windows. Small pieces of trees were scattered across the road, little sticks with clusters of leaves attached, plastered to the pavement. The ditches on either side of the road were running with muddy water. I slid around the corner from Millbank onto Gera Road, went off the road a little and dented the quarter panel of my car.

The rain was driving hard and I could barely see, the wipers uselessly pushing water around. I almost missed my driveway, I was going so fast. I banged and splashed through the mud and struck the Caddy a glancing blow. For a second I'd have sworn there were several soldiers in the yard as my headlights swept across it, but I barely registered them. I heard the shots and saw the flashes through the downstairs windows. The car came to a skidding halt in the mud, and I skipped the steps and shouldered through the half-open door, the Remington slick and cool in my hand, my heart like a Diesel engine throbbing clear through my neck and into my temples.

Nestor Lazos was stretched out on the floor, his body twisted around in an unnatural position, blood pooling from a crater in his chest. His automatic pistol lay a few feet away where he'd dropped it as he fell, his hand a gnarled claw forever to remain empty. His green eyes were already drying out like week-old grapes, the sightless stare of the dead.

The porkpie hat was still screwed down on his head.

Ethel was sitting on the floor, not blinking, the shotgun still smoking in her white-knuckled grasp. She looked tiny, as if she were shrinking away from what she'd done.

"Are you hurt?"

She looked at me as though I were a phantom, as if she wasn't sure I was there.

"Ethel are you hurt?"

She shook her head, a small, nervous movement. I took the gun from her, opened the breech, and ejected the shells. She'd hit him with both barrels.

"We'll get the sheriff," I said.

She stared at me, pale, shaking. I put the gun down and sat with her, held her like her life depended on it. She put her face in my chest and I put mine in her hair and we sat there like that, holding onto each other, an island in the cold grey world.

It was some time before either of us was ready to move. When we got ourselves together, we went and got John at home and asked him to dial Spruce 2049 for us. He did, and the sheriff said to give him twenty minutes. It was closer to half an hour before Powell made it out to the house, uniform and hat and not a hair out of place.

After the doctor had examined Nestor's body and they'd packed it up and the sheriff had taken all his notes, he put away his book and his pen and said, "you figure Lazos here was looking to repay you for what you did to his buddy?"

"Would it matter? He broke in the house and tried to hurt Ethel."

"Where were you, Cogbill?"

It was like my body had been hollowed out. I was an embalmed man walking around under the pretense of life. But Ethel wasn't finished unloading on guys in our living room.

"You know what your problem is, Sheriff? You're bad as my daddy. You look at me and see a little girl. I tell you I think there's a crime going on and you send me away with a pat on the head.

"Then because I done took up with Cogbill you figure he's no good and you don't listen to him neither. I'm a grown woman, I do as I please. Hieronymus is the only one who seems to understand that. You want to apologize to me, you better get in line."

The sheriff knew when to walk away. When the last of the vehicles had left our driveway, we stood looking at the mess on the floor.

"He's right, Ethel. This was my fault."

"Cogbill, you need to stop throwing yourself down every available flight of stairs. You're aware how I feel about you, quit trying to change my mind. Why not accept that you can be happy like other people?"

"I'll only let you down."

Old quick-draw Burkitt hauled off and slapped me again.

"Never say a thing like that again. I told you once I didn't want to be part of your penance, and by God you will not make me."

"I should have been here."

"Is that what this is about? Not too long ago I asked you to respect me, hell I just got done telling the sheriff that you did. Don't go making a liar out of me now. Do you think I'm with you because I want you to protect me?"

"I was ready to kill Nicky and Nestor and hide the bodies. I really screwed up."

"Is Drakos...?"

"I couldn't do it."

"Then Harry Cogbill you didn't screw up."

"No, I just let you do it instead."

"Come to bed. We'll clean up tomorrow."

"I'll be along."

She gave me a long look and turned, unbuttoning her pants as she walked away. I should have followed her. A sane man would have. But I stayed up and made a half-ass attempt at cleaning up the blood. It wouldn't all come up and I was going to have to sand the floor and re-finish it, or maybe just set the house on fire and start from scratch. I sat in the living room for hours, unmoving. Not even Fawkes would come near me. I spent the night in the kitchen, staring at the clock, drinking coffee, listening to Fawkes make strange noises.

When dawn came I put on my hat and went for a drive. I had no plan. King George County amounted to little more than a crossroads. It had the distinction of being exactly between things: exactly between DC and Richmond, between the place George Washington was born and the place where he grew up; between James Monroe's birthplace and James Monroe's law office; it was even between the Rappahannock and Potomac rivers. In short, it was a place people passed through on their way to somewhere else. Even John Wilkes Booth had the sense to die just across the river in Caroline. But not me. I was out of work and out of money, and I had to find some way to feel worthy of the girl at home, curled up in my bed, strong and fierce and gentle and loving, who believed in me and did not require that I be anything I am not.

I spent the day looking for jobs. Hunting for work is a far less terrible activity than many I have partaken in for the sake of my country, but I would not describe it as pleasant. However, I got lucky. Bob Horne, a businessman from Florida, was about to open one of his 24-hour restaurants and candy shops in Port Royal, just across the James Madison Bridge, and they were hiring cooks. Although I did not intend to spend the rest of my life flipping burgers, it was a job and for a little while, it was altogether better than canning pickles.

It was suppertime before I made it home, and I was half-afraid that Ethel would have left the house, thinking I had run away. But I was a fool to cast doubt upon the divine will. When I arrived at the end of my driveway, Ethel Burkitt was sitting on my porch, drinking a cup of coffee.

"I was starting to think you'd left town."

"I had to prove to myself that I deserve you."

"Hieronymus, I cain't hold all your pieces together. You know that. You told me it ain't my job to fix my daddy, well, I cain't fix you neither."

"When did I ask you to?"

"Some fellas drink. You need someone to love. You don't believe in your own worth unless you see it reflected in someone else's eyes."

"Ethel what are you saying?"

"I thought the language was pretty clear."

"Are we breaking up?"

"I stand corrected."

"Excuse me?"

"Hieronymus H. Cogbill."

"My middle initial isn't—"

"The H stands for hard-headed. Do you know how I spent my afternoon? I brought a roll of chicken wire over here and I made a pen for Fawkes, so he don't have to poop all over the house, and I mowed the lawn, and I think we could make a right nice vegetable garden in the field on the east side of the house, if that's the sort of thing you're interested in."

"You mowed my lawn?"

"It was getting ugly out there, Cogbill. Pretty soon we were gonna be living in a shack in the woods."

"Maybe I like the woods."

"You don't give up on a body just because they cain't walk on water. We're a work in progress. I think that's all anybody ever is."

"I've never met anybody quite like you, Ethel."

"I reckon that accounts for most of your troubles."

"Yes ma'am. I believe it does."

I made supper and a fresh pot of coffee. Ethel had declared it a soup-and-sandwich kind of day, and I took the hint.

The key to a good grilled cheese is to melt the butter first, separately, and then baste the sandwiches with it so they cook up an even golden brown. We had that and tomato soup, and fought off Fawkes' marauding attempts at our food.

"I'd like to put in a doggy door that gives him access to his pen from the house."

"I've been thinking about something like that almost since I got him."

"Think he'll poop outside?"

"Why not? He poops everywhere else."

"I meant exclusively."

"That may take some encouragement."

"Works in progress."

IT TOOK a while for things to get back to normal. I was worried that having to shoot a man would take something away from the woman I loved. And for a time, maybe it did. But Nestor was inhuman, as deserving of being shot as any man had ever been, and Ethel understood that as well as anyone could.

I also worried that my feelings of guilt and shame would poison our relationship. But it was Jesus who said that worrying doesn't add an hour to our lives, and thus the only sensible course was to let go of such feelings. I find this concept difficult to master, but I suppose the important things often are.

One evening after dinner, when we were drinking coffee on the porch and watching the birds forage in the field, I looked over at Ethel and saw her blue eyes peering at me over the rim of her coffee mug, and the lowering sun turned her hair to copper. Words failed me as they always did in these moments, and I realized that my love for her was beyond the reductive scope of human language, and no words, no matter how beautiful or poetic, could hope to express it.

"Marry me, Ethel. Even though I'm old and sorry and can't see the sun for all the light in my eyes. Marry me anyway. Be the one thing in this life that goes my way."

"Don't I always?"

And she did. The days weren't all like the one in Fredericksburg, with the first breeze of autumn in her hair and her arm in mine. But mostly they were good. And when we fought, mostly she won, and I did not mind.

Iris and Elijah Taylor did finally come and visit us. It took several invitations over the course of six months before they accepted. Eventually, Elijah and I sorted things out and even became sort of friends. I give Ethel all the credit for that. I have never been good with people.

We did make Fawkes his doggy door. It took a lot of training but we got him to do his business outdoors, except when he didn't. On the whole I do not recommend keeping a fox as a pet, but Fawkes was a part of our family and we loved him, and his life was a long and happy one.

It turned out the FBI didn't care about Jimmie Vasiliou or Nick Drakos. They were looking at Jerry Drakos, Nick's brother. Jerry was a notorious slumlord who owned a huge amount of real estate in the District. He also leased a lot of office space to various government agencies.

Jimmie Vasiliou and Nick Drakos didn't stack any time. They were sued by L. Thomas Boone of Westmoreland County and forced to sell their interests in the Cloverdale project. Nick died in '74 just before he was scheduled to testify in another fraud suit. The timing has always made me wonder, but some stones are probably best left unturned.

Jack Pope never attempted to recover his land. He also never received full compensation for the sale. The maze of liens was too great for any attorney to spend billable time attempting to unravel. Every developer who touched it lost money. Eventually it was foreclosed and sold at auction. The company that bought it, at a very low price, listed Hector Adagio as its president. The construction continued well into the 1980's, with the finished development renamed Bayberry Estates, bearing little resemblance to the planned Cloverdale Subdivision.

I guess in the end you do the good you can where you can, and accept that ninety-nine percent of what happens in this world is entirely beyond your control. As Ethel likes to say, anything else amounts to jumping in front of a truck and blaming the driver.

Jack died young, and was buried with his mother and father under the trees by Williams Creek, near the site of what was once their airport. The filling station remains in operation, though I'm not sure Jack would recognize it. In 1960, US 301 was expanded to a four-lane divided highway, from the Morgantown Bridge, heading south. By 1964 they'd widened it all the way to the James Madison Bridge, and the traffic circle at Edge Hill was destroyed.

Frank Burkitt died in 1972. Cancer in his mouth that spread to his brain. Nobody knew until it was too late. He never had much use for doctors. You may think I didn't miss him, but that isn't true. He drove Ethel to me, and though he and I never quite saw eye to eye, we did finally find common ground in our love for Ethel, and for the children she bore me. I wish Rollie, Alice, and Frankie had known their grandfather longer than they did.

I have grown old, and I barely recognize King George. Ethel and I still sit on the porch. Once in a while the breeze catches her hair and waves it in the sun and just for an instant, she is twenty-three again and I am forty, and I remember that morning long ago when I thought that I would never know fulfillment or happiness, or the love of a good woman, and then dawn came with the glory of the Lord.

Made in the USA
Columbia, SC
19 November 2020